WHEN YOU FEED STRAYS & GAYS

WHEN YOU FEED STRAYS & GAYS

A Journey of Self Discovery

SHARON GREEN

CONTENTS

Dedicated to Richard France, first lieutenant, USA
Army Air Force, fellow writer, and awesome
father-in-law. RIP

CHAPTER 1

Dr. Kelley

Chuck, Percy, and I were drinking at the bar one Saturday. We were there mostly because we were tired of the same old scenery in my apartment. We were talking the same old crap and getting drunk. We ordered nachos and a basket of barbecue chicken wings. Overall, having a great time. Chuck interrupted a story Percy was in the middle of and made an observation.

"Oh my God!" He squealed, "That's my friend Brad!"

"Go say hi, Chuck. Ask him if he wants to join us." Percy persuaded.

"Oh, I couldn't. I doubt he would remember me." He gasped.

"If you don't think he would remember you, then I would hardly consider him a friend, Chuck," I added sarcastically.

That's where we began to form our genius yet drunken theory about all the people in your life.

Everyone you know fits into a certain category. There are

four categories... Family, friends, acquaintances, and everyone else. Obviously, everyone knows who the first three are. But who is everyone else? That took some careful consideration. We settled in for a lengthy conversation over several more beers. Finally, we came to a unanimous agreement. Everyone else was divided into three sub-categories of their own.

"Thrust upon"- The checker at the gas station who sells you lottery tickets twice a week, your mail carrier, or the old Gray-haired lady that owns the dry cleaners.

"The regulars"- The people you see all the time. Like, say, the lady reading her book at the bus stop across the street from yours. These are people you never speak to but instantly recognize.

"Gone but not completely forgotten."- These are the people you used to know, whose names you may or may not remember, and may or may not remember yours. (Brad fit into this category.)

We thought the whole theory was quite clever and insightful. But that party ended, and we all eventually sobered up. It's pretty safe to say that alcohol can inspire some creative subjects and lead to some odd conclusions. Kind of like the ones I experience in my weekly therapy sessions, minus the beer.

Chuck never did go and say hello to Brad.

There's every possibility that therapy is useless. I don't know if I have benefited from going my whole life or have just enjoyed it. I often think about how ridiculous it is to pay $175 an hour to enjoy chatting with someone. And if she sees that, I don't blame her for keeping her mouth shut. My idiocy is her paycheck.

My love of, or addiction to, therapy began when I was

in grade school. My parents thought my behavior was a bit questionable and decided I needed a psychological evaluation. At the time, it was true, and so did my sister, but she hid it better. The truth about my home life was never mentioned in the sessions. At the time, I wouldn't dare reveal anything. I was scared too. Instead, I made up ridiculous lies to secure my place on the couch. I liked being there. I felt safe.

Eventually, my parents were investigated by Child Protective Services. They were investigating the wrong people, so they never found any wrongdoing. I was declared a chronic liar and had to continue my treatment until further notice. I couldn't have been happier and looked forward to it every week. On Thursdays between 3:00 and 4:00, I would be in my happy place. The only difference now is I don't have to make anything up... I have plenty of fucked up true stories to tell the doctor. All of them thanks to my family, friends, acquaintances, and those people that are gone but not completely forgotten.

* * *

I entered the office through an unusually tall, worn-out, dingy door. It was so cliché; it even had a really loose antique glass knob and rough spots where the varnish had worn off. After I stepped in, I proceeded to cross the room towards an oversized mahogany desk, and the woman with short curly brown hair seated behind it. I think she must have been deep in thought and didn't hear my approach. I couldn't imagine how she didn't hear that funky old door, with its rickety sounds, open and shut.

She stood up from her chair and reached out an extended hand in my direction.

"Good afternoon, I'm Dr. Lynn Kelley. It's nice to meet you!" She greeted me enthusiastically as she shook my hand. "Please take a seat."

"Thank you, it's nice to meet you too," I said and smiled as I let go of her hand and walked over to the crusty old couch underneath the window.

As I approached the well-worn seat, I wondered how many past and present patients it took to dig such deep ass divots in its cracked leather cushions. I sat in the one to the left and let myself sink into the shape of it. The window behind my head filtered in sunlight; it streamed through the dirty panes and reflected itself on the floor in front of her desk; millions of tiny specks of dust swirled in its midst.

"Let's see…." She said while tapping her fingernails on the top of the desk and scanning through my file. "I see your previous doctor was Paul Lewis?"

She had that part right. Doctor Lewis was my previous shrink. He retired recently, and he and his wife packed up and moved to Arizona. He had told me they were tired of the Montana winters. I certainly couldn't blame them for that. I'm sure they're now enjoying a comfortable existence in the warm southwestern sunshine, sipping cocktails by their kidney-shaped pool.

I was sad to see him go and happy for him at the same time. But being the narcissist that I am, I mostly thought about myself and how it would affect me. Starting with a new therapist meant starting over from the very bitter beginning. Would I have the strength?

"Yes, I've been coming to Doctor Lewis for years," I answered, even though I knew she was making more of an observation than asking a question.

She closed my file and laid it on the desk in front her, then folded her hands and placed them on top of it.

"Well, you must have had a successful relationship. I hope we can develop the same in time." Her smile was sincere.

Doctor Kelley told me that when she gets a new patient, she likes to spend the first session together getting acquainted. She said people that feel comfortable around each other tend to communicate better. So that's what we did.

By the time I left, I felt like I could do it. I could start again from the very bitter beginning. It was a chance to tell my old stale stories to someone that hadn't heard them already.

CHAPTER 2

A NEW ROOMMATE

I was halfway down the stairwell to my less than desirable basement apartment when I noticed an unusually large mass looming at the bottom. It was dark, so I stopped to get a better look before continuing. My first thought was that someone's walrus was on the loose. I stood with my eyes squinted, but it wasn't until I heard a meow that I realized it was a cat.

I decided to finish my descent; I could tell he was watching me as I slowly moved toward him. I didn't want to make any sudden moves and scare him. He was sitting on the storm drain next to my front door. Surely, he would make a break for it when I came to close, but he didn't. I found myself standing right in front of him.

"Hey there, big guy, are you lost?" I asked in my calmest tone.

He stood there looking back and forth from me to the front door. I believed he was waiting for me to let him inside. I put my key in the lock. As soon as the door clicked open a crack, he used his huge cross-eyed face to push his way through to the interior of my apartment. I followed him in. This was the biggest cat I had ever seen, one of those brown Siamese ones. He began sniffing everything in his path.

"Sure, come on in!" I laughed.

I stood watching him inspect every inch of the place. I kept a close eye on him, marking this unfamiliar territory would not be tolerated. The fuzzy dice following closely behind him let me know he was a male.

He made his way to the large L-shaped couch left over from the 1970s rec room of my parents' home. It was covered in a stained fabric of green and brown plaid. He leaped onto its side arm with surprising ease. His hefty mass moving gracefully through the air. He proceeded to make himself comfortable. Folding his legs under his chest, lowering his butt, then wrapping his tail around his massive girth. He was there, looking like a huge, overcooked Thanksgiving turkey, one that could easily feed a family gathering of twenty or more. I assumed he needed a place to stay and figured he would be a fairly good roommate. I knew right off that he wouldn't pay his share of the rent. That was something you usually found out later.

I went to Wal-Mart and bought a litter box, scoop-able sand, a litter shovel, cat food, and a few of those fuzzy mice full of catnip. My bowls were already of pet quality, so I used what was in the cupboard for his food and water. He eats out of the Tony the Tiger bowl I ordered off a cereal box many moons ago. I named him Boyd and immediately scheduled his altering for the following Friday.

Boyd is now my best bud. He has his faults, but what are a few scratches on the furniture and an occasional puke pile compared to his unconditional love? I find few of my other friends measure up to him, not that I have many. Some come close; most of them use the toilet, and only a handful have barfed on my carpet. If I had to choose a second-best to Boyd, it would be Chuck.

I sat down to watch my 70-inch LCD boob tube that's mounted on the wall directly across from the L-shaped eyesore. Every Monday evening on channel 66, they have a marathon of "Oldies but Goldies." Eight hours of complete nostalgic bliss fragmented into thirty-minute increments of pure, unadulterated entertainment make Monday TV night. It's also Chuck night.

Just after 7 pm, ten minutes into F-Troop, the door cracks open a touch, and a whiff of Armani floats into the room. Chuck's low but amazingly feminine voice chimes his usual greeting.

"Hell-ooo, my lovely friends, I'm here to grace you with my presence for the duration of the evening!"

He pushes himself the rest of the way into the apartment, grocery store bag filled with the evening's salty snacks in his left-hand six-pack of Diet Coke in the right. Groceries go on the coffee table before he heads for the linen closet and pulls out a pink and yellow floral bed sheet. Chuck's a little apprehensive of the "big L": he finds it to be a bit on the repugnant side. The sheet serves as a buffer between him and the pestilence embedded in the ancient fabric. Once the couch condom is in place, he makes himself comfortable. He won't move for the next two hours and three Diet Cokes. He then takes a seven-minute piss, returns, and repeats. This scenario is exactly the same every week, without fail.

Our evenings are quiet. We focus on the superb line-up. An occasional smart-ass remark is common, especially during the commercials. I watch Chuck licking cheese dust from his fingers, then take a huge swig of room temperature Diet Coke. I don't know why he won't keep it in the fridge... probably because he would have to get up to get another. Not to mention he believes warm soda makes you gassier. He lets out several nauseating guttural burps and tries to mute them with a puffy, pallid, and oversized ladylike hand. It's always the same comment afterward.

"Did you hear that?' Followed by a girlish giggle.

CHAPTER 3

AS FATE WOULD HAVE IT

I remember a fateful night that we shared several years ago. I was half-drunk and ready to go much earlier than the nine o'clock I was scheduled to meet Chuck at his place. Boyd was asleep in my spot on the couch, so with no place to sit as an excuse, I went upstairs a half an hour before he expected me. Chuck lives in the shithole apartment directly above mine. I knocked on the door.

"Come in!" He bellowed loudly, not trying to hide the irritation in his voice.

So, I was a little early. Big deal. I rolled my eyes and pushed my way in.

The first thing you notice about Chuck's eight hundred dollars a month mold garden of a flat is the feminine touches. There's always a large vase of cheap grocery store flowers on his coffee table. Ever-present fresh vacuum tracks in dated carpet scented with Glade "spring rain" are a constant. The air freshener mixes with the ever-present essence of mildew. The smell isn't intolerable; it's just annoying. After a moment or two, the odor disappears into the background. He poked his head out of the bathroom.

"You're so early. I'm not ready yet, so make yourself comfortable" His tone had softened, the irritation was gone.

"Take your time!" I answered, instantly regretting my words. The last thing you want to tell Chuck to do is take his time because he will.

I always feel at home in Chuck's place. He has done so much with so little. Our apartments are anatomically identical, but our decorating styles differ significantly. Chuck's place is as clean as a dump can be and festooned ala inexpensive sheik. Mine could be described as clad in vintage rummage sale, with a touch of cat hair. He tries to convey a sense of elegance in all his rooms. That's not easy on a limited budget, but he does his best to surprise. I notice a poor attempt in the form of a decanter full of brandy on a faux silver tray. There was a group of little glasses sitting around it. I filled one up and took it like a shot. I immediately ran to the kitchen sink and spat it out.

"What the fuck is that shit?!" I said loudly through a gag.

I heard the bathroom door open. "What?" He yelled inquisitively.

"Why do you have a decanter of gasoline in your living room?!" I questioned back.

"What?" He asked again.

"Nothing..." I said dismissively through the sound of the bathroom door slamming.

I grabbed a beer out of the refrigerator before returning to the living room. I drank, snooped, and I started to get bored. It's after nine now, and I'm not early anymore. I decided to make my way around the end table and past the economical yet stylish dining room set to the bathroom overstuffed with all the gay glory that is Chuck. I bounced off the doorframe before poking my head in.

"Will we be going out sometime this evening? I asked sarcastically through a slightly drunken slur.

He turned around to face me. I felt myself gasp, and my eyes widen.

"You told me to take my time!" He sternly reminded.

"Well, I've changed my mind!"

He planted an open palm firmly on his hip. He stood and stared at me as if he were issuing a warning. Despite feeling a little threatened, I had to fight back the urge to laugh.

I wasn't sure how he stuffed himself into that tiny leather skirt or the cropped purple sequined tank. Where the hell did he find men's size 13 stilettos?! He just stood there. Daring me with his sparkly blue eye shadowed glare to comment. Instead of accepting his challenge, I backed up and shut the door; I didn't think getting my ass kicked by a six-foot drag queen would be an optimal way to start the new year.

We had decided weeks ago that we would attend the party at Cool-Jay's for New Year's Eve. They were hosting a fifty-dollar per person "all you can eat." Which included appetizers, well drinks, and cheap beer. It would be quite a celebration, literally a "who's who" of the Missoula gay community and a lip-sync drag show at midnight. It was also within walking or staggering distance. What more could we ask for?

We walked in through the bright red seven-hundred-pound

front door, adorned with one of the tackiest plastic Santa welcome plaques ever manufactured. Chuck loved it. He reached up and used a chubby finger to poke the jolly old elf on the nose.

"Oh, I've got to have this. Remind me to grab it when we leave!" He half-whispered in my direction, then giggled into his hand.

"You are a sneaky little scamp, Chuck!" I said with giddy sarcasm.

It was around 10:30 PM when we finally stepped inside. By the way they were acting, everyone else must have started partying around noon. I understood that Cool-Jay's was a gay bar, but I wasn't aware that "gay" took on a whole new meaning on New Year's Eve. This was to be my first experience waiting for the ball to drop amongst Chuck and all the other girls.

We weren't even three feet in the door before I was grabbed from behind and lifted off the floor. I found myself on the receiving end of an enthusiastic bear hug. It wasn't a good start. I learned later that Tommy had a bad habit of introducing himself by flexing his muscles. His laugh was a hardy guffaw but with a slightly sinister undertone. It startled me. Chuck watched, clapping his hands with excitement.

"Tommy, my love!" Chuck cooed loudly.

They hugged, and Chuck left a kiss-shaped lipstick mark on his cheek. Obviously, they knew each other. Their laughter made me feel a bit more at ease, but my guard remained up.

The evening was turning into a big gay dodging fest for me, but Chuck made himself a target, and a hell of a target he was. He wasn't there to be ignored. This was his night to shine, and that he did! I watched him in awe. He practically floated around the room. Never missing a beat between heart-felt kisses and exaggerated air hugs. Yep, Chuck was walking on sunshine.

On the way home, Chuck hooked one arm around mine and carried the Santa plaque under the other. He needed the extra support; the drunkenness and the stilettos were challenging his stability. We exchanged our regular drunken banter, but Chuck's topics differed from mine.

"Did you notice the guys at the back table? Oh my God! They were so cute!" He gushed, grabbing a tighter hold on my arm.

"There were guys there?" I teased.

We continued to walk and laugh. We gave each other a playful nudge.

Obviously, we had different things on our minds at the party. He was looking for love in all the wrong places, and I was looking for dip without soggy chip butts in it or a piece of celery without a lipstick-stained bite mark.

They put out some clam dip at one point, but it seemed runny and had an odd color. I saw some of the guests double-dipping and swore off the chip table. The hair on my sweet and sour meatball left me no alternative but to nibble at only pretzels the rest of the evening. God only knows where they had been previously, but each handful I grabbed was dry and didn't require dip. I'm not sure what kind of beer was in the free keg, but I drank my fair share. Since I was pretty screwed up before we even arrived, they could have served piss, and I wouldn't have noticed. It wasn't until I spontane-ously yawned that I thought to check the time. I really had to concentrate on the number lit up on my phone. I squinted and finally decided it read 2:48 AM.

Things became fuzzy and split in two. I struggled to see straight but to no avail. Chuck let go of my arm and stumbled on ahead, mumbling about Percy. Percy's his casual boyfriend and, according to him, a real sweetheart. That was the last thing I heard Chuck say that evening.

I heard and felt something heavy strike the back of my head. My legs instantly failed me; I went down like a rag doll full of cement. My head had landed on my upper arm, narrowly missing a curb. I was conscious but frozen with a mind-numbing pain. I tried to get up but couldn't move a muscle. I could only lay there and listen. Descriptive noises informed my mind's eye of an unbelievably horrific scene. I struggled to make my eyes cooperate but could only manage to get them open into small slits. What I managed to see was very blurred, almost as if looking through the bottom of a pink glass. There must have been blood in them.

I could barely make out three figures. They were clustered around a mass on the ground that I knew was Chuck. They were brutalizing him, kicking, punching, and cutting. He was curled up in a fetal position, screaming, crying, and begging for them to stop. I tried to yell at them, but only a guttural groan followed by a cough and some blood came out of my mouth. I had never felt so helpless or completely vulnerable. It was a living nightmare, mostly for Chuck. I passed out.

When I came to, the first thing I managed was a scream. Chuck lay sprawled out completely naked about two feet in front of me. He was covered in blood from head to toe. His face gashed and swollen. His hair plastered flat against his head with sticky, drying blood. He had a multitude of deep cuts and was covered in dirt and loose gravel. They had stuffed a large clump of the hair from his wig into his mouth, and his clothes were strewn about. They had severed his penis. The Santa plaque lay smiling beside him. I was sure he was dead.

The lights went out again. The next time I came to was in a hospital emergency room. When I opened my eyes, they were instantly assaulted by the fluorescent lighting in the room. My head was pounding, almost as hard as my heart. My thoughts raced to Chuck.

The nurse told me Chuck was in critical condition and had been flown to Harbor View in Seattle. My whole body flooded with relief at the fact he was still alive. He was one tough motherfucker.

I was bandaged and invited to stay the night. They must have wanted to make sure my head wasn't screwed up any more than usual. It took a few days to find out Chuck would make a recovery. The word " full" was not included. I'm assuming because certain things don't grow back. He spent a few weeks in the hospital. After his release, he stayed on in Seattle for nearly two months. His mother lived there. She took care of him until he was well enough to come home. I thought that was the best thing for him. What a better time to have your mommy?

We talked and texted every day. He told me that they never found his penis. I felt a bit queasy when he half-jokingly suggested a stray dog or cat probably got to it.

Chuck popped open a fresh warm Diet Coke and took a big swig. Boyd stepped up onto his belly to investigate the can. Chuck let him sniff the opening, then leaned forward to kiss the feline's inquisitive face before blasting it with a huge, forced burp. I had to smile. McHale's Navy was just starting.

CHAPTER 4

SHIT HAPPENS

Dr. Kelley tells me that my friends reflect my own personal preferences, ideas, and morals. I couldn't disagree more. In fact, it may have been one of the heftiest loads of bullshit I'd ever heard.

I believe friends happen to you. You don't have the luxury of shopping for them. They aren't hand-picked. They just happen. Randomly pick a friend in your mind. Where did you meet them? School? Work? While you were out socializing?

Did you pick any of them out of a catalog? I'm guessing probably not.

Sometimes you even like the people you are thrust into friendships with. Other times they just fit the circumstances of your life at a given time. Often you kind of like them, or not at all. If you spend enough time with them, they can grow on you, possibly like a cyst, wart, or a cancer.

Once you have certain friends, you learn that they are also split into categories over time.

The first category would be "best friends." aka, the close ones. Those special people that you would do anything for and can tell anything to with confidence... And vice versa.

The second category would be "fun friends." You know, the ones you call when you're having a party or want to go drinking. Pretty much any social situation.

The third category would be everyone else that is a "step above acquaintance." Donna and Jerry came to mind.

I met Donna and Jerry under unusual circumstances. It was nobody's fault that our lives collided. I could have sworn I looked behind me, both over my shoulder and in the rearview mirror. Jerry swears he did the same. As fate would have it, we both pulled out of our Safeway parking lot spaces simultaneously. Unfortunately, they were across from each other. No real damage ensued, for which I was quite grateful, due to the fact that I had just borrowed the car from a friend for the day. After a brief chat, we amicably parted ways. I noted as I pulled away that they seemed like a nice enough couple. Our time together in life was both brief and pleasant...as a fender-bender encounter could be.

Three months later, we met again purely by chance. Every summer in Missoula, there are a variety of festivals that take place. One in particular, "The Testicle Festival," is a favorite of Chuck's, occurring at the end of July. We attend every year. We walk around eating strange greasy festival cuisine and drink as much beer as we can. Occasionally, there are strange and random sex acts that you're welcome to witness or ignore. It's a something for everyone kind of event.

We were waiting in line for a Rocky Mountain oyster

when I spotted Donna. I had one of those "I know her, but I don't remember from where" moments. Then I noticed Jerry, and it all came back.

"Hold our place, Chuck. I'm going to say hi to a couple of friends and will be right back." At that point, I should have said acquaintances, but I didn't feel like being so nitpicky that day.

They were several people ahead of us in line. I wondered if they would recognize me. I walked past the procession of testicle lovers to the vendor's order window menu. I pretended to note a few prices and turned to walk back to Chuck and our place in line. I intentionally made myself discernible. I dropped my keys as I was walking past them, then bent over slowly to pick them up. It worked. Jerry had a broad smile and an extended hand.

"Well, fancy meeting you here, stranger!" He said in surprise.

I accepted his shake and gave Donna a hug.

"Donna, Jerry, this is my friend Chuck. Chuck, this is Donna and Jerry." They exchanged hellos and handshakes.

We ate deep-fried bull balls together at an incredibly dirty table in the blazing sun. Our lower-end friendship was born.

Donna and Jerry grew to be known as "the couple," not that they always acted like it. Their relationship seems perfect to the unknowing eye. To those who are blessed to know them, perfect would not be an adjective of choice. They are truly two people who can't live with or without each other, but they should consider giving it a shot.

A few of us took a weekend trip to Las Vegas. Chuck, his sweet boy Percy, Donna, Jerry, a friend of theirs named Gina, and me. Thank God it was a quick trip. Who knows what more would have happened if we had stayed any longer?

I'll cut to the chase. We did some touristy bullshit, what we could squeeze into two and a half days. One show, four buffets, a lot of drinking, and gambling to taste. It was a group effort, for the most part.

Jerry and Gina decided to spice things up a bit. Honestly, I saw it coming like a freight train. The trip started out on an upbeat and energized note. We all expected a fun and exciting time.

After a group gorging at the Monte Carlo buffet, we decided to drop fifty dollars each into those buck a spin machines. We figured at a George a pull; someone was bound to score a decent hit. We were correct. Percy hit and made seven hundred dollars right off the bat. He opted to take the money and run, obviously as bright as he is sweet. We didn't see him or Chuck again until we boarded the plane home.

I lost my fifty in four minutes, which is typical for me. I wasn't all that concerned. I'm what some would refer to as quite comfortable, but I stopped at that loss. I'm also considered by many to be a bit frugal, but the truth in plain English would be that I'm as cheap as any asshole out there, maybe even cheaper.

Donna was doing the button-pushing on the machine. It was one of those that had different sequences of sevens and cherries. Jerry stood behind her, watching for the big pay-off. Jerry's a tall and lanky guy with green eyes, dark hair, and no ass. One of those poor bastards you feel like walking up behind to pull up his jeans. He's not a good-looking guy. Not the type of guy you would expect to see with Donna. Donna is striking; long copper hair, blue eyes, petite, slim, and well dressed. They say opposites attract, and in this case, it appears to be true. I wondered how she could stomach sleeping with him. Don't get me wrong, Jerry's a fun and likable guy; but he looks like he could have been the dude voted least likely to get laid in high school.

I noticed Gina was cruising around, watching others gamble. She is a decent-looking woman with short dark hair and blue eyes. I must say, though, she has an ass that could shade half of Texas, shapely yet titanic. From the moment I was introduced to Gina, I sensed something was off about her. As it turns out, I was right.

When I saw her approach, Donna and Jerry, I had a hunch and hung back a bit, taking it all in. She glanced my way and gave me a smile that conveyed she didn't care that I was watching... or if I saw what she was going to do.

I was only half surprised when her hand slid across Jerry's ass (what he has of one). I was fully disgusted that he didn't seem a bit fazed by it. He only put a wandering finger behind him and hooked it to one of hers. As I watched, I felt my eyebrows leap closer to my hairline. I wanted to yell to them sarcastically. "You do see Donna sitting there, don't you? You pathetic turds!" But of course, I didn't. I think at that moment. Jerry may have slipped off of my "just above acquaintance" list.

Jerry leaned over slightly to give Donna a peck on the cheek. Completely absorbed in her two dollars per spin progress, she didn't seem to notice them walk away together. Gina glanced over her shoulder at me as they were leaving. I flipped her off when she winked at me.

I took the vacant stool next to Donna. We spent the next half hour laughing at wins and groaning at losses. She decided that eight hundred dollars was enough and pushed the collect button. We went to the cashier window to reap her rewards. I accepted her offer of a drink at the bar.

I noted how strange it was that she didn't mention Jerry even once while we chatted. She seemed distracted and looked around as if she were searching for something or someone. I knew the signs and why she was agitated. She was feeling Jerry's absence, and you could tell it wasn't sitting right with her. She finished off her gin and tonic, pushed her glass of ice, holding a squeezed-out lime wedge towards the middle of the table. She sat and stared at it as if in a trance. Suddenly snapping out of it, she looked up at me.

"I'm gonna go up to our room and take a little nap."

With that announcement, she stood and started walking towards the elevators, patting my shoulder on her way by.

"OK, I'll see you later." I called after her.

I lost a few more bucks on the slots, took pleasure in another buffet, and bought a keychain shaped like the MGM Grand lion. I couldn't find a shot glass with the name Boyd etched on it. Then I realized how stupid it was that I even thought to look. On that note, I decided to go to my room and take a little nap myself before embarking on my continued bender at the Hard Rock Cafe.

I resumed the bender, but I never made it to the Hard Rock. When I stepped off the elevator on my floor, I stood still for a moment to decide which direction to go. This happened every time I went out, there were a few different elevators that went to the same floor, and I always picked the wrong one. All the hallways look the same, so it's kind of like completing a maze to get to the room. Soon after picking my path, I realized I had chosen the right one.

Donna was sitting with her back against the wall, outside her and Jerry's door. She looked up at me as I approached. She was visibly shaken, but there were no tears. Standing beside her, I looked down, and she met my eyes.

"Jerry's in the room, but he's busy at the moment." She blurted in a resentful tone.

"Oh geez…" Was all I could think of to say. I extended a hand to help her to her feet. She reached up and accepted my assistance.

We went into my neighboring room. My first reaction to any sign of adversity, turmoil, or conflict is to pour alcohol. We each cracked a beer fresh out of my bathroom basin filled with cans and cold water. The water was a lot of ice this morning. I like to plan ahead.

She took a seat at the small table in the corner by the huge window covered with blackout drapes. I sat on the bed up against the headboard that I had stacked pillows in front of. I clicked on the lamp beside my bed and settled in. She pushed back the edge of the curtain and peered out at this bustling strip below. We just sat in silence, enjoying the quiet.

Once she started her tale, it was like the floodgates opened. She spewed forth much more than I ever thought I would know about any two people's relationship. Six beers later, she took a breath. She studied me through squinted eyes, head cocked to one side, waiting for my input.

There were probably about a million things I could have

said to her. And out of those million things I could have said to her, I chose the worst thing of all.

"What are you gonna do?... I think the first thing I would do is cut off his dick and shove it down Gina's throat!" I cheered in support.

I watched her eyes widen, and her hands tightly grip the arms of her chair.

"What the fuck does Gina have to do with this?!" She demanded.

My body instantly tensed with panic.

"Oh my God!" I spewed through the hands I had pressed tightly over my mouth. I sat and stared at her, afraid of what might be coming next.

She slammed her beer can on the floor. It was half empty and erupted a gush of foam when it landed with a thud. She charged for the door, gripped the handle, and pulled it open violently. She turned back in my direction and thundered hysterically before making her exit.

"He's dead. He's fucking dead! It was bad enough that I thought he was in there with a hooker!" She yelled in some kind of scream slash grunt.

I just sat there and listened to the heaviness of the door click shut behind her.

I turned on the TV, making sure the volume was up high enough to mute any noise that came from the neighboring room. I didn't want to be involved in a murder trial. If I couldn't hear anything, I thought I might be able to use plausible deniability as an excuse not to.

I decided I was exhausted. I had drunk enough and spread enough joy for one day.

I woke up wondering if my neighbors were still alive, and if so, would they be interested in a final buffet before going to the airport? My bags in hand, I knocked on their door.

Jerry opened it a crack. I asked if they were ready to go. He gave me a look I didn't recognize. He ran an open palm from the middle of his face to the top of his head.

"We'll meet you downstairs in about 45 minutes." He said flatly before shutting the door in my face.

I headed out for my final buffet. It was delicious yet bitter-sweet. I sat and waited an additional twenty-five minutes for them to show up at checkout. I had decided I would leave for the plane after thirty. They finally showed up looking quite sober. Gina was nowhere to be seen. We got a taxi and barely made our flight.

I was making my way down the aisle, trying not to bump too many elbows with my carry-on. Chuck and Percy waved and smiled from their seats way in the back of the airplane. The sight of them made me smile. I waved back and took my seat. Thank God I had two normal friends.

Donna and Jerry made it home together, intact as a couple. We never saw Gina again or ever mentioned her. I guess what happens in Vegas really does stay there.

CHAPTER 5

A REALIZATION

Dr. Kelley suggested we talk a bit about my lifestyle. She was aware of my inherited wealth, as well as my substantial case of thriftiness. At first, I wasn't sure where she was headed with this. It ended up going down a road I wasn't too keen on traveling. I could literally sense the pending questions.

"Why is it that you don't work? She asked with genuine interest.

"Well doctor Kelley, I feel, and please correct me if I'm wrong, I feel as if I would be taking a position away from somebody who actually needs a job."

I was exultant with that answer; I thought it made me sound somewhat noble. I wasn't quite sure if she bought it, but I stated it so well, and with such confidence, I almost did. Then she retorted.

" I wasn't aware that jobs were so scarce." She commented with an obvious air of sarcasm.

Thank God, she didn't push it, I was feeling a bit embarrassed already. Then came the hard question.

" Have you ever considered volunteering? I'm pretty sure there are plenty of openings...."

"Well... you got me with that one," I confessed in shame.

I had no other choice, I had to come clean. I described my shortage of motivation and my abundance of laziness. Until I heard myself say the words, I wasn't aware what a selfish asshole I really was. I guess she woke me to a personal reality.

I couldn't help noticing her nose wrinkle as if she suddenly smelled a fart. Her eyebrows dipped down in a poorly muted look of disgust. I started doing some obvious fidgeting. I could feel the heat rising in my cheeks, both sets. I was fairly sure I was forming a sizeable butt crack sweat line on my seat to be noticed when I stood up. I decided to scooch around on the chair in an attempt to wipe it up, or at least smear it, so it would dry faster after I left.

She composed her expression before she went on to explain.

"Helping others not only benefits the community but can raise one's sense of self-worth and personal satisfaction. I think you could benefit greatly from it." Her eyes squinted as she smiled.

I sat slightly bobbing my head. I held my face in a look of serious consideration.

She made several suggestions on how I could serve the community. I could volunteer at the old folk's home... or clean cages at Animeals, a local animal shelter, and food bank. Shop for the disabled? Pick up litter in the local parks? Help at the homeless shelter? Pick the noses of those with no fingers, wipe the asses of the populace afraid of fecal matter, and on and on, and on and freaking on. At that point, all I wanted to do was get the hell out of there. Dab the excess moisture off my ass and change my underwear.

I learned a couple surprising things about myself that day. I was a self-centered, lazy jerk... and my ass sweats profusely when I'm put on the spot.

CHAPTER 6

RECRUITING CHUCK

Chuck and I were having a few drinks at Curley's happy hour. I realized he was getting awfully close to being completely shit-faced. Soon I would be able to make my move.

He grabbed a cigarette out of the pack sitting in front of him and popped it in his mouth. Even after noticing he had inserted the wrong end, I let him continue. The lighter clicked, and he touched the flame to the butt, searing the filter into an unusable lump.

"Fuck!" He swore and pulled a few stray tobacco bits off his tongue.

"You know damn well you can't smoke in here, Chuck." I reminded.

An annoyed server bussing a station across the room was glaring at Chuck in annoyance.

"It's OK. I got it!" I announced through a smile and a wave of my hand.

He nodded and continued wiping down the table.

Of course, the incident sparked the whole public smoking debate. Chuck didn't seem to care that I was agreeing with him. He argued with me anyway. Then he tried to suck the people at the neighboring table into the dispute.

He looked in their direction and loudly slurred.

"Don't you think if you own an establishment, you should be the one to decide if people can smoke it?! HA! I mean IN it!"

He found his faux pas quite amusing and continued to belly laugh.

They pretended not to hear him and continued minding their own business. He looked back at me and shrugged his meaty shoulders. I decided this was a pretty good time to change the subject.

" Say Chuck. Doctor Kelley wants me to start volunteering somewhere." I blurted, desperate to pique his curiosity. He just sat there, looking at me through a blank stare. I continued.

"She said it would improve my self-esteem and self-worth, you know, bullshit like that. So, I've been giving it some thought and decided it might be something to consider. I was hoping that maybe we could find something together."

His expression remained uninterested.

"This is where the old saying misery loves company comes into play, right?" He offered in a bland tone.

"Yeah, I guess you could say that," I admitted

"I can see it now." He said, waving his plump hands in circles in front of his face like he was conjuring an image.

"You and me, up at 5:00 AM every morning, in your tiny

kitchen, making sandwiches for the homeless. We pack them lovingly into paper lunch sacks decorated with Hello Kitty!"

After a long snort, a huge swig of beer, and a rancid burp, he continued, and I let him.

"We could add snack bags of Doritos and airplane-sized bottles of scotch!... Oh, oh, and on special occasions, we could throw in a snack pack pudding cup! Maybe even a plastic spoon!"

He pounded his fist lightly on the table to accentuate his laughter.

"Fucking smartass," I said, laughing myself.

He agreed with a nod and another gulp of brew. We continued to laugh. It's pretty amazing what booze can disguise as funny.

"Come on, Chuck, will you do it?... Come on, man. Throw me a bone, for once!" I practically begged.

"OK, OK! I'll do it. I know I owe you one." He agreed reluctantly.

I gave him a slightly inquisitive look, accompanied by one raised eyebrow, after his response.

"One?"

The only problem now would be if he remembered our agreement tomorrow.

The next morning, I woke with a gigantic mass of brown fur sprawled across my neck. I pried Boyd off my airway, yawned, and recalled the inebriated previous evening. I guessed Chuck would be in one of two places. Hungover in a jail cell in downtown Missoula, or a big gassy blob sprawled out on the big L.

I headed out into the front room. I was relieved to see

his fat, snoring ass fast asleep, face down on the couch. Boyd walked ahead to investigate. He put his front paws on Chuck's shoulder and began licking his ear with a sandpaper tongue. Chuck pushed the cat away with his open palm.

" Buzz off, Boyd!" He blasted under his breath.

He rolled over with a loud fart and a strained grunt, then hoisted himself up into a seated position. He looked up and offered me a small hung-over smile.

I went into the kitchen and grabbed a Diet Coke.

"Here, this ought to help," I said as I handed it to him.

"Thank you!" He gushed as he accepted it with a sense of urgency.

He took a huge swig, followed by an astonishingly long, deafening burp. I knew what was coming next.

There would be a lineup of morning-after questions. Mixing Chuck and alcohol in no way adds up to total recall. He started with the usual. "Did I meet someone? Did you meet someone? Did we go to Taco John's? "I told him we didn't meet anyone or eat anything. He breathed a small sigh of relief.

Then I reminded him that he agreed to volunteer with me. He took another gulp of soda. I think he incorporated the word fuck into his second gut-busting belch. The noise prompted Boyd to retreat back to the bedroom. He stood up and walked toward the bathroom.

"You're a fucking asshole. I gotta take a dump."

We were on our way to community service.

CHAPTER 7

ORIENTATION

I carefully considered the list of places Doctor Kelley had suggested I volunteer at. My lack of interest in any of them prevented me from deciding. So, I called Percy and asked if we could meet and talk. Since he knew Chuck as well, if not better than me, maybe he could make some suggestions. We met for lunch at Outback Steakhouse. I was sitting at the bar when he arrived.

"What's up buttercup?" He giggled, as he climbed onto the bar stool beside mine.

"Has Chuck mentioned to you anything about he and I doing some volunteer work?" I asked.

"Oh yes, I gotta tell ya, he's pretty excited to find out what you'll be doing!" He informed enthusiastically, grinning from ear to ear.

"Are you kidding?" I asked.

"Well, of course I'm kidding, you know Chuck better than that!" He said and poked me with his elbow.

Percy ordered the Asian chicken salad and a glass of white wine. I ordered a French dip sandwich and a vodka 7. We chatted over our meals.

"If I, were you and Chuck, I would hang up the list of options and throw a dart at it." Percy suggested only half-jokingly.

We finished eating and took our drinks into the bar. Percy threw the dart. Blushing Meadows it was...

I met up with Chuck later that day for dinner and drinks. We were having a good time and didn't want to go home, so we walked around downtown Missoula. We stopped into just about every bar we passed. I decided not to talk about anything that might bring down the mood, including volunteer work. Tonight, was for relaxing and blowing off a little steam. We would pay the piper tomorrow.

The following morning, I struggled up the outside staircase to Chuck's apartment. Knocking politely before letting myself in. I passed through his tidy living room on my way to his bedroom. I was quite sure of the scenario I would be walking into. A huge snoring, sweaty lump, concealed in 1800 thread count Ralph Lauren bed sheets, and the stench of Skyy vodka mixed with stale rancid farts. It was an accurate prediction. I gave him a firm poke on the shoulder. Nothing ... It crossed my mind that he could be dead. Then he snorted and rolled over. He opened his bloodshot eyes, wincing. Just the reaction you want when you're the first sight of someone's day.

He greeted me with a raspy and productive cough. Then he asked me what the fuck I wanted. I sat down on the edge of the bed. My weight caused him to roll towards me. His mid-drift spare tire bounced onto my thigh.

"Wanna go have breakfast? I'm payin'." I enticed.

No hangover in the world would keep Chuck from a free meal. I knew that for a fact. We sat down at a semi-clean table in Ruby's cafe. Chuck was wearing his sunglasses. They would remain on throughout the entire artery-hardening repast. I was glad. The last thing I wanted to see was his bloody, un-interested stare while I explained our new volunteer duties. I attempted to eat my runny egg yolks but thinking about his eyes made my stomach turn. Guess I was a little hungover myself, but I pressed on.

What do you do with a drunken fag? Thanks to Percy and a random dart, he was about to find out.

"What's Blushing meadows?" He inquired, not bothering to conceal his disinterest.

"It's a home for older folks and people in need of convales-cent care."

Chuck's initial reaction was less than enthusiastic.

"Why don't we just scrap all this volunteer bullshit?" He complained through a mouthful of ketchup drenched hash browns.

He wanted to back out. I reminded him of his promise to escort me on my journey to self-improvement. I could smell the hate and alcohol secreting out of his pores. I wasn't going to let this fat fucking fish off of the hook. He was gonna follow through on something. I was going to benefit; he was going to benefit, and all the patients at the home were going to benefit. All our lives would be fuller and more meaningful from the experience; God damn it!

We walked through the heavily smudged glass double doors together. The unpleasant smell hit me first; my nose involuntarily scrunched towards my eyebrows. Chuck gave me a look, not a friendly look. It was one of those short, warning-packed glances, my skin crawled.

We made our way up to the reception desk. A skinny, old ugly woman was seated behind it. She gave us an unwelcoming stare. I wanted to grab Chuck by the sleeve, turn and run. I didn't, but I probably should have.

Chuck folded his huge feminine fingers into a proper pile and plopped them in front of the old bitch and her outdated computer.

"Hello Ma'am, we have an appointment to meet with the director for volunteer orientation today!"

His cheerful confidence continued. He assured her that we were there to help in any way necessary, and we were happy to do so. I wasn't sure whether to puke, laugh or applaud.

She picked up the receiver of an outdated push button phone and selected a line.

"They're here." She said simply and hung up.

A few moments later, we were being led down a long hallway. We came to a stop and were abandoned at a door labeled "Director". I felt nervous and anxious, the way I used to feel as a child getting ready to walk into the principal's office. Chuck tapped the frosted glass of the door window lightly with his knuckles.

"Come in," A voice bolstered from within.

Chuck turned the knob and pushed the door open. He walked in with confidence, as I practically tiptoed behind him. A small gray-haired man was sitting behind a gigantic desk. He looked like a sweet little grandpa. Looks can be deceiving.

Chuck once again took the initiative. He strode forward, with his hand extended towards the directors' desk. His gesture wasn't reciprocated. I wasn't sure if I should be embarrassed or pissed off. Chuck dropped the intended handshake to his side, at once launching into an obviously aggravated semi-composed introduction.

"Good morning, Sir, my name is Chuck Barnes, and this is my..." He was cut off midsentence by the irritated sweet little grandpa.

"I know who you are! Sit down over there." He demanded as he pointed to a row of chairs that lined the wall. We complied.

I noticed a little fire rising in Chucks plump cheeks. Despite his irritation, I could tell he was gathering his composure. I admired his self-control.

He cleared his throat before he continued. He spoke like he was reading a memorized list. He gave reasons explaining our interest in volunteering at this fine establishment. His spiel was full of creative and insane compliments, peppered with fabricated concerns for the elderly and disabled. It was all complete bullshit.

I knew he was doing it all for me. I was reminded of why he was my best friend. I definitely needed a reminder from time to time. As touched as I was, I didn't try and interject. I skipped any form of assistance. I was ashamed of myself but decided to live with it.

Marvin Quinn listened to Chuck's banter without interruption. When he was sure Chuck was finished, he opened a heavy desk drawer and pulled out a worn clipboard.

"Follow me." His voice strained as he stood from the desk and reached for his walking stick.

He hobbled towards the door, clipboard under his armpit and a well-worn cane in his shaky aged hand. Chuck offered me a condescending smile before turning to follow Marvin, the miser. We were about to experience a well guided reluctant tour of Blushing Meadows Nursing Home.

Sundays would never be the same.

CHAPTER 8

DENNY'S

I arrived early at Doctor Kelley's office Last Thursday. I walked up to the reception desk in the lobby of the building. As usual, Teresa was sitting behind it, smiling as she watched me approach.

"Good afternoon, you're early today!" She observed cheerfully.

"I know, I'm running early today, but I figured I could just sit and wait."

"That's not a problem. Go ahead and wait in her office. That way, you can fix yourself a cup of coffee. I'll let her know you're in there when she comes back from her errands."

"Thank you." I smiled and headed for Doctor Kelley's office.

Once in, I went straight to the Keurig machine. I wished I had checked to see if there was vanilla creamer before brewing a cup because there wasn't any.

"How the fuck am I supposed to drink this without creamer?" I asked myself in my best annoyed tone.

When I think back on myself walking around her office, searching frantically for a way to dispose of this undrinkable coffee before she enters the room... I kind of have to laugh. Why do I act like such an idiot? All I had to do was tell her I couldn't drink my coffee black. I think she would have been fine with that. But no, what do I do? I pour it into the plant sitting in the corner. I embarrass myself, even when I'm alone. I dropped the paper cup into the wastebasket and took my seat on the well-worn couch.

The door opened and made a creaking noise that matched its appearance. She walked in and shut it behind her.

"Hi there, how are we doing today?" She chimed.

"Oh, pretty good, I got here a little early, so I thought I'd just sit and look at my phone until you got here." I lied.

I couldn't imagine telling her the truth, but the thought of it made me smile.

She hung up her coat and purse, then situated herself at the desk.

"So, have you looked into any volunteering possibilities since we last talked?" She asked through a tight smile.

I sensed she was expecting a slew of excuses as to why I hadn't. When I told her yes, I had, her expression was one of possible disbelief. I felt internal smugness. In case I forgot to mention it earlier, I can be a bit of an asshole.

"Wonderful! Did you find something you'd be interested in?" Her expression turning sincere.

"Interested in" wasn't exactly the description I would have come up with. I explained to her that I recruited Chuck to join me on my volunteering adventure, she responded with an impressed arching of the eyebrows.

I told her about Chuck's initial resistance to the entire idea but had agreed to it because he knew he owed it to me. Then I went on to tell her about how impressed I was by him, how he stood up for the both of us in the adverse situations we encountered. I described the way he handled Marianne at the front desk and the director Marvin, the miser. I told her I couldn't believe he had it in him to take the bull by the horns and handle it with grace.

Then my story kind of went south on me. She cut off my Chuck praising and began questioning me about how many of my friends, past or present, have let me down. She wondered why I was so surprised by being supported by someone who I considered a best friend. It caught me off guard, not that she asked, but that I hadn't realized it was such a foreign experience.

She struck a note in me. I realized none of my friends ever have stepped up for me. But on the same note, none of them had ever thrown me under the bus either. That was a whole other session. I did have memories of people that screwed me over pretty well, but none of them were friends. I wondered if she cared about the other categories of assholes. One in particular suddenly came to mind.

A few years ago, I had a day all to myself. It started with sleeping in until about 10:00 AM. Then I went ahead with the usual daily routine, not to be skipped. I filled up Boyd's Tony tiger bowl, scooped his litter box, picked up furballs, and cleaned up puke spots. I didn't feed myself because I planned on having lunch out that day.

I was sitting in a booth at Denny's, waiting for my order. I enjoy eating at Denny's, it's cheap, and they never try to rush me. I had forgotten the newspaper and had already read the carte de jour. So, I decided to people watch and eavesdrop instead.

I quickly noticed these two guys in a booth across from me. They were skanky looking bastards, to say the least. They weren't nearly as quiet as they should have been, considering the content of their conversation. They bantered back and forth about the price of an ounce of pot that some other asshole had brought back from Seattle. Keep in mind that at the time marijuana was illegal.

Anyway, I was distracted by the waitress refilling my watery coffee. She was a sizable woman with an ass to match. She was blocking my view. There was no seeing around her, so I had to be patient.

"There you go, Hun; can I get you anything else?" She said pleasantly as she administered the top off.

(Ya, you can get your fat, friendly ass out of my way.)

"No, thank you. I'm fine," I returned with a cheerful grin.

Coffee pot in hand, she waddled away.

I could see four hands under their table doing a very fluid brail like exchange. Nice and smooth boys, except for the fact that I saw the whole thing. They got up and left the table. I could smell the stench of body odor, pot, and stale Marlboros in the wake as they passed by.

They left the chunky server a huge mess and no tip. What a couple of cheap assholes. There I was, just sitting there feeling sorry for the big butt waitress because she didn't get a tip. I should have been more concerned about the two boils on the ass of society that just made a drug deal in an American institution like Denny's.

Truthfully though, to my admitted shame, there was a time when I wasn't considered much better. Maybe I'm still not... but I'm a good tipper. Today I'm probably just more cautious or too chickenshit to take the chances the youth find no big deal. With that realization, Billy came to mind. Billy and I shared a horrific and unforgettable night. I lost my appetite and couldn't finish my Superbird sandwich as I recalled it in detail.

CHAPTER 9

BILLY

Billy was by far the biggest fucking asshole I had ever met. I was going to say in the world, but I hadn't met all the world's fucking assholes. So, dubbing him the biggest would almost be giving him an honor. Honors were not something he deserved. Billy was the kind of guy anyone would have loved to see get his throat slit. I'm sure more than a few individuals considered doing just that.

Billy's girlfriends always had a black eye or some other sort of facial abrasion. As big a prick as he was to them, he always seemed to have one. I guess there's no shortage of chicks with low self-esteem.

Billy was also a believer in and practitioner of animal abuse. He had a dog named Bruce. Without going into the whole sordid story about Bruce, I will just cut to the happy ending. One night Billy got his ass kicked, and Bruce was stolen from Billy and went to live with a very nice family in a neighboring city. The end.

I could go on all day about the horrible things Billy has done, but who needs to hear it? Just trust me when I say I don't think you would have liked him.

The two of us met about fifteen years before through a mutual acquaintance. At the time, it seemed a necessary union. Billy had the best shit a die-hard smoker could ask for. Don't get me wrong; the pot wasn't for personal use. I already had plenty of bad habits under my belt. I smoked cigarettes, drank like a fish, ate like a pig, and swore like a sailor. Enough is enough. Besides, the cost was ridiculous. That was why Billy and I formed our twisted alliance. I saw the opportunity to profit from the pathetic addictions of those willing to pay anything for just one more hit. I became the "middle-man, profiteer extraordinaire."

Billy's girlfriend at the time was named Allison. She went by Ally. She was a gorgeous girl with mousy brown hair and beautiful big green eyes. Usually, one of which was encased in a ring of black. I didn't understand her attraction to that stupid prick. I'm guessing she may have questioned it a time or two herself.

The three of us met one evening for a lot of drinks and for what could potentially be a mutually lucrative business deal. We sat at a table in the corner of the bar. I instantly noticed the band-aid perched over Ally's right eyebrow. I shook my head slightly and laughed to myself in honor of the sheer idiocy of their relationship. We talked about unrelated bullshit, ate deep-fried chips dipped in a slightly discolored guacamole, then downed about eight shots of scotch each.

We got down to business. Billy decided to tickle my

frugality bone. He convinced me to buy a substantially more significant amount of product than I had initially intended. He explained how the larger quantity would lower my investment price, thus increasing my overall profit by as much as a fourth. I was sold. The new plan required going for a ride.

We piled into Billy's rust-riddled 1972 ford pick-up. Ally sat in the middle, singing loudly to a Dolly Pardon song barely eking out of the static-ridden radio.

"Jolene, Jolene, Joleeeene!" She crooned with her eyes closed. She sounded pretty good.

"There's a cooler full of Coors behind the seat. Somebody grab us all a can!" Billy called out over Ally's inspired singing.

I reached behind the seat and flipped up the cooler lid. Reaching in, I felt a lot of cans but zero ice. I didn't say anything, just grabbed three cans and passed them out. We all cracked one open. Nobody seemed to care that they were piss warm.

I was nothing short of astonished by the fact I was having a good time, not something you usually experience around Billy.

The ride was far from smooth. Between the shitty shocks and abundant potholes, we did some serious seat leaping and laughing. It's amazing what becomes funny when you're full of scotch and tepid beer. We hit a bump that sent Billy's Coors can crashing into his top teeth so hard we were sure it had become a permanent dental fixture.

"AHHH! Son of bitch!" He yelled as he reached for his mouth.

Ally laughed until warm Coors was oozing out of her nose.

"Shut up, you stupid bitch! It ain't funny; it hurt like hell!" He yelled as he swung his arm and smacked her face with the back of his hand.

Then I think she may have switched to crying. It must have hurt. She recovered quickly and resumed drinking. Once again, I just kept my mouth shut. I was here to do business, not to perform an intervention.

We saw the striped arm of the railroad crossing was in the upright position and preceded to cross. A dizzying wave of panic washed over me when our back tires wouldn't clear the tracks. There wasn't a train coming, but just being stuck on the tracks was enough to scare the hell out of us. It was the same kind of feeling I got when somebody yelled "Jaws!" while I was in the swimming pool after seeing the movie as a kid. I just wanted to get the hell out.

I opened the door and got out of the truck, lit a cigarette and walked around to the driver's side. His window was open.

"What do you think? Should we try pushing?" I asked with a certain amount of panic.

"I don't know. This suckers pretty fucking heavy." Billy said as he got out and walked toward the back of the truck. I followed.

He grabbed the tailgate and gave it a shove.

"It's not going to happen." He said in defeat.

Not willing to accept his word at that point, I stepped up myself and gave it a push.

"Shit!" I yelled. He was right.

"I'll call a tow truck," Billy announced and pulled his cell phone from his shirt pocket.

I saw a beaming light coming towards us from a long distance down the track. The striped arm suddenly came down and landed on the truck bed. Red lights began flashing. It was surreal and seemingly out of nowhere.

" OH FUCK!" Billy screamed as he took off running, knocking me off my feet in the process. I fell hard onto the railroad tracks, my elbows breaking my fall. I crawled to the open passenger door and struggled to pull myself up. Ally was still sitting in the middle of the bench seat.

"Ally! Come on! Give me your hand. We gotta get out of here!" I screamed at the top of my lungs.

I reached in and grabbed her hand, and pulled as hard as I could. She was frozen in complete shock. I continued to scream at her and tug with all my might. The beam was upon us, and it was too late to save her. I jumped away as far as I could and landed on my back. I covered my head with my arms and used the little strength I had to roll farther away from the impact.

I bet it's safe to assume that those pretty green eyes had never been that wide open before. She must have been paralyzed by her fear and a lot of less than premium alcohol.

The impact was unparalleled. I had never heard a noise like it before, hope I never do again. I knew I was alive only because I turned my head to see the sight of my life. There were sparks, smoke, and fire. The screeching of the train brakes and steel scraped along steel was deafening. I must have passed out. When I came to, it was quiet, except for the sound of sirens far away in the distance. I lay still, crying and listening to the emergency vehicles grow closer.

I'm not sure how I managed to get to my feet. I did a lot of staggering as I walked towards the wreckage. The train dragged the truck at least a few hundred feet down the tracks.

My perception and judgment were less than fine-tuned that evening. I felt like I was getting close when I fell, hard. My face took the hit that my hands should have. I used all the strength I had in my arms to lift myself enough to pull my cheek off a protruding rock. It didn't seem to hurt; I must have gone completely numb by then. I rolled myself onto my ass and just sat there a few more minutes. At least it felt like a few minutes; not sure.

As I sat, my vision began to clear; I hadn't even realized it was blurred. I leaned forward to prepare to stand again. My left hand landed on something soft. I looked down to discover it was resting on what resembled another hand. I screamed and fell back. It was small and had lovely pink fingernails, and a petite jade ring on the index finger, not unlike the one Ally was wearing that evening. As I followed my natural line of sight, I noticed the hand was connected to an arm. A partial torso and a neck followed. No head. I wondered what had happened to those beautiful green eyes. My head was spinning, and I threw up.

I woke in the ambulance, paramedics looming over me. I could smell vomit inside the oxygen mask they had strapped to my face. They asked me questions. Not sure if they were supposed to do that. I couldn't answer anyway. I still can't believe that in the midst of all that horror, confusion, and sadness, I could lay there with selfish, trivial thoughts.

I was glad that I hadn't given Billy any money yet. Can you believe that?

Several years after that fateful night, I saw Billy again. He didn't see me. I watched the stupid fucking jerk sit alone, eating a Wendy's hamburger with one hand. His right arm was missing from the shoulder. I knew it didn't happen in the accident. That pussy was probably snuggled up in his bed before the train struck the Ford. I really hoped that cocksucker was right-handed.

CHAPTER 10

OFFICIAL FIRST DAY

I was feeling apprehensive as I leaned against the front of the building. With every second that passed, I was convinced I was being stood up. The positive part of my brain told me that Chuck was a good friend and he would never let me down. I imagined seeing him come bounding around the corner at any second. Then there was the realistic part of my brain, telling me a different story. Chuck was narcissistic, selfish, and a lazy asshole. He wouldn't think twice about blowing me off to sleep in. Then I was pissed. That son of a bitch wasn't coming! Then panic set in. What if he didn't show? Could I walk in and fulfill my obligations alone? After all, I had dragged him into this situation just so I wouldn't have to do it alone. I leaned my head back against the brick, regretting that I hadn't brought my cigarettes. I was feeling a bit too close to an anxiety attack and decided to flee the scene. I wasn't halfway down the cement stairs when I heard his voice.

"Good morning! I'm here! Are you ready to spread some joy today?" He chimed loudly in his most exaggerated gay voice. He pranced towards me, waving his plump hands wildly.

I smiled and waved at him as he approached and scolded myself internally. Why the hell hadn't I decided to leave just a few moments earlier?

I turned around and went back up the stairs. I pulled open the heavy glass door and held it for Chuck.

"Are you ready for this?" I asked him in a hesitant tone.

"You bet your ass I'm ready!" He winked as he walked past me into the building.

Our first Sunday at Blushing Meadows began with force-feeding octogenarians and quadriplegics nutritionally balanced breakfasts. After which, we were handed bus tubs and transformed into cafeteria custodians. I was hoping for an early dismissal, but it wasn't to be. Our last task was to pay a friendly and stimulating visit to a lonely old lady. That sounded easy enough.

Carole Stapleton lived in room 212. She would be our assigned resident. We were to visit her every week for an hour before leaving the home. They told us that Carol had spent the previous 15 years inside room 212. The past ten of which had been without a single visitor. It became obvious quickly as to why...

The door to her room was slightly ajar. Chuck tapped on it lightly as he pushed it open. I followed him in.

"Good morning, Carole!"

Chuck greeted the old woman sitting in a wooden chair

beside the window. I thought it odd that the chair didn't have a cushion. I'm always noticing stupid crap like that.

She was tiny, her hair pure white and short. It hosted a few remnants of an ancient perm. As we entered her domain, she turned her attention from the outside view to us. The lack of cushion allowed her to glide easily in our direction. She looked at us as intruders. I guess we were.

"Who the hell are you?!" She demanded.

She not only sounded like Katherine Hepburn but also had the slight head bob.

Chuck continued with his recently assumed role as the initiative taker. He rushed towards her; arms open wide.

"We're your newly assigned weekly visitors!" Chuck explained as he embraced her in an "air" hug. That's a hug where you put your arms around the subject without actually touching them, except for a light finger tap on the back. She wasn't digging it. Then he grabbed her hands on his way back to an upright position.

"You are just the cutest thing I've ever seen!" He declared enthusiastically.

I'll never forget or be able to describe Chuck's face when she pulled her hands away as abruptly as a 90-something crone could manage.

"Keep your big queer mitts to yourself, you jackass!" Her head bobbed wildly, and her fists clenched tightly.

I couldn't help but let go of a snicker. Chuck glanced back at me with a look of warning. It made me laugh again. He pursed his lips to hold back his own burst of laughter. He turned back to Carole.

Chuck let forth his most profuse apologies. I could tell

she was enjoying his embarrassed nervousness. After a bit of cajoling, she agreed to let us stay and chat for a while. By the end of our allotted hour, we knew a hell of a lot about Carole Stapleton. It seemed she was in the mood to let us in on every miserable moment of her life, from conception to the present day.

Carol was born to a pig farmer, Archie, and his wife, Anna, about 400 years ago. They had immigrated to Anoka, Minnesota, from Norway about 300 years before that. Carol told us that the shit of her life hit the fan from the first memory in her head. This crazy old bitch was one for the books. I had wished Doctor Kelley was there to hear all this. As apprehensive as I was, Chuck seemed enthralled with her ever so fucked up American story.

In a nutshell, Carole's father had been an alcoholic and indulged in several extramarital affairs. According to his wife, most of them were with various prized livestock. Her mother, on the other hand, had been a staunch Christian. Both a Bible beater and a child beater as well. The story became garbled to me; my lack of interest, disbelief and sheer disdain at Chuck's undivided attention made me sick.

She shared her reasons for the lack of visitations. My ears perked up. Carol had six children. The paternity of those individuals was in question and obviously, at this point, would remain so.

Carole's firstborn was Sarah. Carole described her as one of the ugliest girls she had ever seen. Hence, she was quite relieved, nay, overjoyed, when Sarah found someone to marry, a man named Raymond. He was equally challenged when it came to looks. They were on their way to a new life together in Eugene, Oregon, when they were both killed in a head-on collision. Carole shrugged her shoulders and added nonchalantly,

"It was probably for the best; their children would have been nothing short of beastly."

Chuck's eyes widened at her comment, and I actually heard myself gasp. If she noticed, she didn't seem to care and continued.

Jeffrey was her second child. He was born only ten months after Sarah. Carole said she was overjoyed that he was a handsome baby. Unfortunately, he turned out to be what she described as a full-fledged retard. Jeffrey was institutionalized at the age of 5 and died of pneumonia at 14.

Chuck's eyebrows furrowed, and his look became intense. I tried not to laugh; it was tough.

Tessa was the third in line of utter catastrophe. She was a beautiful, active and intelligent child. She managed to live to the ripe old age of 17. Carole doesn't recommend ice fishing to close to the spring thaw. Tessa succumbed to the cold, attempting to save herself on the slippery edge of ice she had fallen through. An autopsy concluded that there was no water in her lungs, proving she had died before she slipped under.

Ella and Andrew were born together. They would have been numbers four and five had they been live births. I thought about how lucky those two were.

Caleb was the last inauspicious infant to emerge from the old bags' loins. I was happy to hear that, to this day, he is alive and well. Although according to Carole, he's an ungrateful little bastard that doesn't feel the need to visit his poor old decrepit mother, rotting away in a nursing home. She didn't elaborate on it. But I can imagine he is probably a decent guy with a life of his own…and doesn't need the grief of a crazy, old miserable bitch of a mother telling him how lucky he is to be alive.

Before she could break into another unbelievably disturbing story, I reminded Chuck of the time.

"We need to get going now Chuck," I informed him, then turned my attention to Carole.

"It was nice meeting you, Carole, our time's up for today, but we'll chat again next Sunday," I told her through what I could muster of a smile.

I thought it was brave of Chuck when he dared to pat her on the knee while saying goodbye.

"Thank you for the amazing stories, Carole! We'll be back before you know it! Take care, dear."

She must have taken a shine to him because she smiled and waved as we left.

"Goodbye, Chuck; thanks for visiting!"

She knew I noticed that I got no mention. She glared at me momentarily, her head bobbing a little faster than normal. Chuck closed the door behind us. I began to laugh. Chuck gave me a playful shove from behind as we headed for the exit.

We stopped at McDonald's on the way home. We decided to get our food to go to watch TV and eat on the couch. I was so happy to walk through the front door. I was exhausted. Fast food bag in hand, I headed for the Big L and collapsed onto it.

"I'll get us a couple sodas," Chuck said as he headed for the kitchen.

"Aren't you tired at all, Chuck?" I called after him.

He came around the corner holding a Diet Coke for each of us. I accepted the tepid can and popped it open.

"Yeah, I'm pretty tired, but I feel great. I think we actually made a difference today! I can't wait to go back!" He gushed with excited sincerity.

Besides my urge to puke, I was happy for him.

Boyd appeared from the bedroom at the sound of Chuck unwrapping a cheeseburger. I sat and watched them as they competed for the tasty sandwich.

I couldn't believe Chuck loved his volunteering experience. I couldn't help being a little jealous and annoyed by it. Chuck was experiencing what Dr. Kelley had intended for me.

CHAPTER 11

THURSDAY

It was unusual for Dr. Kelley to be in her office when I arrived. Pushing the door open a crack, I peeked in. She was at her desk clutching a coffee cup, the way you would if your hands were cold. She turned to look in my direction and gestured me forward with a wave of her hand.

"Welcome back!" She chimed through a sincere smile.

"Thank you!" Was my witty retort.

I headed for the Keurig machine sitting on a small table in the corner by the filthy old window. After swirling several sugar packets and a generous dousing of vanilla creamer into my mug, I was ready for our session. As I went to my seat, I realized it wasn't there anymore. The old leather couch with my forever imprinted ass niche was gone. It had been replaced by a new tan faux colored suede, wooden armed, factory direct, piece of cheap shit. I about dropped my cup.

"I got a new love seat, isn't it nice? The old one was about shot."

"As I eased myself down onto its unfamiliarity, I answered, trying to hide my disappointment.

"Oh, it's nice."

It was as hard as a cement park bench. This was going to make for a difficult session. In fact, my hatred of change could be a session all in itself. I would try extra hard to stay focused.

She took a long audible sip of her coffee and set the mug down on a dog-eared People magazine. She looked up at me with a smile on her face. She folded her hands and place them in front of herself on the old worn desk. I've come to recognize this as her listening position. Today we were going to have an in depth and analytical discussion about my new career as a volunteer. She had a look of anticipation and genuine interest.

"So, how are things going for you and Chuck at Blushing Meadows?" She was practically beaming.

This was going to be hard. I wanted to tell her the truth but was afraid it would make me sound like a total asshole. I sat and pondered for a minute. I was pretty sure no matter how I described it, I wasn't going to come out looking to good.

"Well, Chuck really enjoyed it, but I don't think it's my cup of tea." I felt myself wince slightly, in anticipation of her reaction. She sat back in her chair; her smile faded. Her face took on an expression of question and concern.

"Can you explain to me what you mean exactly? Are you saying you didn't enjoy the experience?"

I decided that I couldn't sugarcoat this. I was just going to have to tell her like it was. There would be no mincing of words. I would just admit it... I'm a total asshole.

I wasn't exactly sure where to begin my tale. Should I start with the extremely rude staff and how we were made to feel completely unwelcome? Or should I explain to her right off the bat that I didn't care about Blushing Meadows or its residents. I didn't like how they all smelled. I didn't care if they ate their geriatric mush or if they fell off their chairs. I didn't like their wrinkly old skin, all their rashes or their outdated polyester pants covering shit filled diapers. I didn't like it. Any of it. Could I even begin to explain Carol Stapleton? I had never met such a miserable old bitch in my life. Every syllable that came out of her mouth was offensive and unbelievable. Probably why Chuck hung on her every word. No thank you to all of it. I wanted to spend my Sundays on the couch with my cat and the fucking remote control.

That was pretty much how I presented it to her, minus the swear words. When I was finished with my unflattering summation, I sat back in silence, waiting for my tongue lashing. Instead of letting me have it, she simply took a deep breath and held her composure. She readjusted her seat and refolded her arms. She leaned forward and cocked her head to the side before delivering what she undoubtedly thought was great advice.

"What if you found a cause that you would be more interested in and have a bit more compassion for?"

I told her that under normal circumstances, that would be a good idea. But it was totally out of the question. I had a much bigger problem than Blushing Meadows. In a word, Chuck. I couldn't even imagine telling Chuck I wasn't going back. I had to push, pull, drag, bribe, and threaten him into joining me to volunteer in the first place. He may be a fag, but he's a big fag. A big fag with a big temper. Besides, he's my best friend, next to Boyd, and should not to be bailed on. I was the instigator of this fucking mess, and I was going to have to see it through. Hopefully, Chuck would lose interest overtime, his obsession with collecting manufacturers coupons lasted less than six months.

While Dr. Kelley disagreed with continuing to take part in something I hated so much only to please Chuck, she understood and didn't argue. Next, she suggested that I should try and change my attitude. She urged me to have a discussion with Chuck. It was possible that trying to understand his point of view would help me. Then she came up with a real zinger.

"What if you were to imagine that Carol Stapleton was actually your grandmother? Do you think you would have more compassion for her?" She asked in a sincerely caring tone.

"No, the only thing that would do, is make me want to puke, kill her, and kill myself! I blurted in jest.

She didn't seem to appreciate the humor. She tried a few more suggestions which I found equally ridiculous. I began to lose interest as she rambled on and on. My mind slipped away...

I wondered if you could microwave a whole chicken, if you browned it on all sides in a frying pan first? But why would you bother? It would be much easier just to throw it in the oven at 350 and wait an hour. Geez. Wait, what if your oven was broke...then it would be a legitimate question! What in God's name is wrong with me?

CHAPTER 12

NOT A FAN OF CAROL

Later that evening, I was sitting on the couch watching TV with Boyd. About 6:30, the door swung open, and all of the glory that is Chuck, bounded gleefully into the apartment.

"Hello my lovelies! He used a sequined sneaker to push the door shut behind him. "Would we happen to have some leftovers from dinner?" With that, he carried his warm six-pack of Diet Coke to the kitchen table and set it down with a tinny clunk.

"We had hot dogs and Kraft macaroni and cheese. The leftovers are in the fridge. I think there are a couple buns by the toaster."

He clapped his puffy hands in an applause of approval. He proceeded to microwave the fare and pull a plate out of the cupboard. Soon he was seated at the end of the couch. He made his usual 'mmmm' sound as he chewed his first bite of wiener. After shoving a large forkful of reheated macaroni into his mouth, he decided to inquire.

"What are we watchin'?" A few stray halves of chewed noodles landed on his lap.

"Oh, just some documentary about overweight gay men that habitually mooch off of their friends."

"Oh my, we're wearing our silly pants today!" He giggled and swung his head to the side to move his bangs out of his eyes. He reached over me and grabbed the remote off the edge of the couch. I didn't protest. I had a much bigger task in front of me. I was going to make a full confession to Chuck about my feelings concerning Blushing Meadows and Carol Stapleton. I decided to wait until he was done with his food. Then I would break out a bottle of vodka. Chuck has always been a happy drunk. I hope today is no exception.

As soon as I noticed chuck's plate was empty, I offered to take it into the kitchen for him.

"Oh, thank you!" He had a look of great surprise as he handed it to me. It was something I didn't normally do. It didn't seem to tip him off that something else was coming. I grabbed a couple of clean drink glasses out of the dishwasher and filled them with ice. I put a shot of Skyy vodka into each of them. I filled mine to the rim with 7UP and Chucks with Diet Coke. I used my finger to mix them before returning to the living room. I sat them on the coffee table in front of us, then sat back and watched as Chuck flipped through the channels. He squealed when he landed on the Bravo channel.

" A Project Runway marathon! "Oh my God, I haven't seen this in so long, must be my lucky day!"

I was less than excited to spend the rest of the evening

watching 18 years of amateur designers trying to impress a bunch of snooty judges. But I was going to do it, at least until Chuck was drunk enough to be interrupted.

About halfway through his fourth drink, he announced that he had to take a piss. I was encouraged to see a little sway in his walk as he headed for the bathroom. This meant he was close to being primed. A few minutes later, when he returned, he was carrying the floral bed sheet he used to cover the couch.

"Get up for a minute. I want to spread the sheet on the couch."

"Don't you think it's a little late for that? We've been sitting here over an hour already." I said as I stood up.

"Yeah, well, I had lost my mind momentarily. I was thinking more about dinner when I came in. At least if we cover it now, maybe we'll only get a mild case of dysentery instead of the full-blown kind."

"What fuckin' ever, Chuck," I said with an eye roll.

He fussed with the sheet until it covered the rancid monstrosity to his satisfaction. I didn't say anything, but I did like it better with the sheet on. I didn't have to think of all the cat hair, dander, petrified food particles, and whatever creepy amoebas were lurking in its fabric. He finished his task and plopped back down heavily onto the couch's Downy fresh softness. I could see a question form on his face as he turned to me.

"Do you think maybe sometime this week we could go couch shopping? I know you have enough money for one. Why are you such a cheapskate?"

I couldn't think of a reason not to, except that I hated shopping. As if he had read my mind, he added.

" You know, I could go shop around for you. Percy and I could make an afternoon of it. We both have excellent taste!"

It dawned on me that I could score some points here. So, with as much enthusiasm as I could muster, I answered him.

"Sure, that would be great! I'll even treat the two of you to lunch as a thank you for your efforts!"

His eyes lit up, and he began stamping his feet frantically in excitement.

"Yippee, I'm so happy! After this episode, I'll call Percy!" He concluded his display of pure joy by blowing me an air kiss.

I smiled and nodded. If he didn't see through that load of bullshit, he must be drunk. I decided to face the inevitable and start the Blushing Meadows discussion. If he hadn't been sitting right next to me, I would have signed the cross.

"Hey, Chuck?"

He turned to look at me. The sight of his content expression unnerved me a bit. I knew things were about to unravel for the evening. He waited patiently for me to continue.

"Look, Chuck, I need to tell you something," I said in such a way that made the statement sound like an apology. He lowered his face and lifted his eyes to me. It was what he did to give me his " What the fuck are you talking about" look.

"I'm not having a good time volunteering at Blushing Meadows. In fact, I can't stand it." With that, I lifted an open palm in his direction, almost as if it were a self-defense gesture.

"But before you say anything, I promise I'm not quitting. Please just hear me out, OK?"

He continued glaring at me, but he complied, and I continued.

"How would you feel about requesting a new resident to visit? Carol Stapleton absolutely disgusts me. I'm sorry to say that. I know you like her but being in her room is like torture for me."

"Are you kidding?! Carol is one of the most interesting people I have ever met!" He half yelled in complete disbelief. "You just don't understand her!"

That's where I about lost it.

"Oh, I think I understand her! She must be the original spawn of the devil! Chuck, she's happy her children are dead!" I caught myself and lowered my voice before I continued.

"Look, Carol just isn't going to work for me. It's up to you if you would like to continue your visits with her. But I'm going to have to move on. You know things aren't going to work out when you fantasize about killing someone!"

It caught me completely off guard when he started to giggle and asked me through the hand he had covered his mouth with.

"You actually have fantasies about killing her?" He let another snicker slip through his fingers.

"Yes, and pretty damn often!" I stated as seriously as I could.

"OMG! tell me how you kill her. Is it the same way in every fantasy? He asked with way too much enthusiasm and amusement.

"You're fucking sick. You know that, Chuck?" I told him, relieved that the mood had shifted in a good direction.

I decided to indulge him with my tales of gore. He hung

on every word as I described all four ways Carol Stapleton met her demise. He then agreed to dump Carol and request a new resident. I was more than satisfied with the outcome of the evening. But I soon learned that different isn't necessarily better.

CHAPTER 13

EEECK!

It was 6:45 when I woke up. My alarm was set for seven. I hate when I'm forced to use the word fuck as the very first word of the day. 15 minutes? Not nearly enough time to go back to sleep, and just long enough to want to continue laying there. So, there you have it, fuck.

I turned the alarm off to preempt its blast of obnoxious, shrilling beeps. They scare the hell out of Boyd daily, without fail. I laid there the full 15 minutes, petting my comatose cat, and dreading the day ahead. I watched the longhand click onto the 7. I felt compelled to swear again as I threw back the covers.

I shuffled across the room and arrived at the bathroom. I reached around the door frame and flipped on the fan and the light. I stepped in and stood in front of the mirror over the sink. I stared for a moment assessing my face, my nose scrunched up in disgust. I decided I probably just needed to clean the glass.

I side-stepped in front of the toilet, turned around, and took a seat. It only took a moment for me to realize that I should probably retrieve my book from off the lid of the toilet tank. I opened my copy of Jaws to chapter 8, where I had left off after yesterday's epic dump. Things moved along much more smoothly than I had expected. I hadn't read nearly as much as I had allotted time for, so I remained on the porcelain rim until my ass was getting sore. I decided to dog-ear the page after Chapter 12.

I slid open the left panel of the frosted glass shower doors. As I leaned in to turn on the hot water, I noticed I wasn't alone. My eyes opened as wide as physically possible, and my breath suddenly drew back into my lungs. It was a big fuckin' spider. I hate spiders. I would have been happier to see Freddy Krueger. With a little more might than necessary, I slammed it shut again. I leaped to my feet and grabbed my greying white terry cloth robe from the back of the door, and made a frantic exit. As I tied the belt and sinched it way to tightly, I stood and tried to rein in the exaggerated panic I was feeling. I knew I was acting ridiculous.

I walked over to the edge of the bed and studied Boyd. He was in a deep sleep, sprawled out like a lifeless body. Maybe he could help me out. How many times have I witnessed him chasing bugs? He loved it; I never saw one escape his wrath. Spiders are bugs, aren't they? Of course, they were! But to be fair and buy myself a couple minutes, I decided to Google it first. I went to the other side of the bed and grabbed my phone.

Me: "Are spiders bugs?"

Google: " No. Spiders are not insects... insects fall under

the class Insecta while spiders fall under the arachnid class. An insect has six legs, two compound eyes, three body parts (head, thorax, and segmented abdomen), two antennae, and generally four wings."

Me " Fuck you, Google!"

I dropped my phone back onto the side table and practically flew around the bed. I scooped up Boyd's limp body. He instantly tensed up as he awoke. Upset and startled, he began struggling to be freed. I tightened my grip on him and forced him into the bathroom, and kicked the door shut behind me. I lowered him to the floor. I walked slowly back to the shower. I don't know why I was trying to be quiet. I guess just in case he had the ability to hear me coming and be on the defensive. Yes, I'm an idiot.

Slowly I slid the door open a crack and peeked inside. It was still there and hadn't moved. I looked down at Boyd. He was sitting by my leg, looking up at me with his inquisitive, crossed blue eyes. I gradually pushed at the slider until the opening was wide enough to accommodate his plumpness. Nonchalantly, I bent over and picked him up. I cradled him in my arms, kissed his face, and scratched under his chin. If I hadn't known better, I would have sworn he was looking at me with suspicion. I carefully placed him on the cold porcelain tub bottom. I pointed out the intrusive arachnid. It took a moment, but he finally noticed it.

He walked over and sniffed carefully. It didn't move. With a slow and steady paw, he gave it a careful tap, and the motherfucker jumped at him! I let go of a high-pitched scream, and Boyd launched halfway up the shower door with his legs scrambling to find the traction to escape this evil setup. He made his exit and bolted past me. He ran for the door but had to stop because I had shut it. He turned around and glared at me. I slammed the shower door shut again. I felt horrible.

"Oh, buddy! I am so sorry!" I practically wailed as I approached him. My intention was to pick him up and hug him apologetically. Needless to say, he resisted my advance and clawed at the door. I opened it and let him bolt. He ran straight for the living room and began scratching the hell out of the couch. Maybe this is the way people learned things before Google existed.

"Hey, Chuck..." I said into my cell phone in a slightly desperate tone.

"Are you about ready to get going?" He asked eagerly.

"No, not yet; I have a little problem going right now. Can you come down here?"

"OK, what's going on?"

"Can you just come down, please?" I requested a bit to impatiently.

I could only imagine his eye roll as he hung up the phone. It wasn't but a few moments later that he pushed open the door and entered with his usual exaggerated style.

"What the fuck is going on down here? We're going to be late!" Was his greeting.

"There's a huge, and I mean HUGE fuckin' spider in my bathtub!" I blasted angrily. "It even scared the living shit out of Boyd!"

"Oh crap..." He replied through a twisted grimace.

I took him into the bathroom so he could look at it. He resisted, understandably.

"Just take a look, Chuck, I want you to see what I'm up against, please?" I practically begged.

He took hold of the towel rack and pushed the sliding door open, ever so slightly. One quick peek in, and he slammed the door shut and gasped.

"Let's deal with this when we get back from Blushing Meadows. I'll call Percy while we're there. He has a friend that studies all different kinds of bugs. He can bring him over." He suggested while he gently pushed me backward, out the bathroom door.

"He studies bugs? I don't want it analyzed; I just need somebody brave enough to step on it!"

"I know, I know! Let's just let him handle it, ok?"

I agreed reluctantly, and we headed out. So many things we're going through my mind. But what worried me most was that it wouldn't be in the tub anymore when we got back.

"Spiders aren't bugs," I informed him as I shut the door behind us.

We were less than five minutes late when I pulled open the heavy door for Chuck to enter the reception area of Blushing Meadows. Chuck had baked a variety of cookies the night before. He headed straight for the front desk and laid them heavily on its surface. Marianne stood and looked at him with her usual stoic disinterest. He was quite excited as he explained to her.

"Good morning, Marianne! I stayed up last night and baked chocolate chip, oatmeal Raisin, Molasses, and sugar cookies for everyone! I thought about making peanut butter too, but didn't want to run the risk of anybody being allergic.

The last thing we need is an outbreak of anaphylactic shock!" He joked.

She didn't laugh or even smile. She just gave him a small nod of approval and took her seat behind her outdated computer. I stepped forward.

"Hi Marianne, I was wondering if I could talk to you for a moment?" I asked in an inquisitive and friendly tone.

She didn't say anything. She just glared up at me in annoyance.

"We, well I, was wondering if I could pick another resident to have visiting time with. I don't seem to get along with Carol Stapleton all that well." I stood looking at her waiting for a response, with a stupid smile plastered on my face.

"Why the hell would I care what you do?" She said flatly and turned her attention back to her task.

My initial reaction was to be pissed at her rudeness but quickly changed my mind. I decided to go with relieved that she didn't care. I turned to Chuck and shrugged my shoulders. I waved my hand in the direction of the commissary. Chuck picked up his tray of cookies, and we headed towards its entrance.

After wiping the last of the gruel from all the solemn, wrinkled little faces, Chuck made an announcement.

"Everybody!... Everybody!" Chuck chimed loudly while clapping his hands to get their attention.

"I baked cookies for everybody!"

Half of the residents turned to look at him. I'm not positive, but I think the other half just didn't hear him.

"We will be coming around with a tray, and you can select

what kind you would like" With that, he slipped on a pair of flimsy clear plastic gloves. He turned to me with a request.

"Would you be a dear and go get some of those little white plates from the kitchen, the disposable ones on the top shelf by the refrigerator? " I smiled and complied.

When I returned with the little white disposable plates, we began the distribution. We were quite pleased that everyone seemed happy and enthusiastically chose what flavor they liked. The tray was almost empty before Mrs. Smyth decided to spit on it instead of making a selection.

Chuck arranged the rest of the spittle sprayed cookies on one of the small plates. He placed it on Marianne's desk as we walked past it on our way to our next assignment.

Chuck insisted that we make one last visit to Carol Stapleton together. I agreed. Just knowing it was my last time in that room was enough to get me through it. Next week I would be visiting Walter Brower.

CHAPTER 14

SAYONARA CHARLOTTE

We stepped off the bus onto the sidewalk, and our eyes were instantly assaulted by the bright afternoon sun. Chuck overreacted in his usual style. His hands flew up suddenly to shield his eyes.

"Oh my God, it's so bright!" He gushed in exasperation and began rubbing them with his fists.

"Yep." I agreed and started off toward home. I was probably more than ten paces ahead before he noticed I had started walking.

"Wait for me!" He whined as he waddled quickly to catch up.

"I'm starving! What should we have for dinner? He inquired excitedly.

"I don't know Chuck. I'm a little more worried about the mammoth spider in my tub right now!"

"Oh shit, I completely forgot about that!" He apologized through a disgusted wince.

"I take it that means you forgot to call Percy?" I asked in an inquisitive and annoyed tone.

He pulled his phone out of his pocket and placed the call. I could faintly hear Percy enthusiastically answer.

"Hi doll! Are you busy right now?"...No? Great. I was wondering if you could call your bug expert friend?... We're having a bit of a problem. When we left for Blushing Meadows this morning, there was a great big hairy spider in the bathtub. It even scared Boyd.... Oh, that would be great! Call me back if you get ahold of him; thanks, see you in a bit." With that, he slipped the Android back into his pocket.

We opened the door to the apartment and stepped in feeling quite apprehensive. I walked into the kitchen and laid my keys on the counter. Boyd was on top of the refrigerator, peering down at us. My first thought was maybe he was hiding from the spider. Normally he would jump down when I got home. I looked at Chuck and could tell he knew what I was thinking.

"Do you think it's still in there?" He whispered.

"God, I hope so!" I gasped.

"Should we take a look, or do you think we should wait for Percy?" He more suggested than asked.

"I think we should look. If he's still there, then we can relax in the living room without wondering."

He agreed, and we walked slowly to the bathroom door. We stood for a long moment before turning the knob. Chuck had a horrified look on his face, which I didn't find reassuring.

I slowly pushed the door open a crack. Suddenly there was a loud knock on the front door. We both jumped, and Chuck screamed. I felt like I was going to have a heart attack. I slammed the door back shut.

Chuck opened the door and invited Percy and Nathan into the apartment. As freaked out as I was, I found myself smiling at the sight of the "bug expert." He was a tall nerdy looking guy with wire-rimmed glasses that hosted freakishly thick lenses. His hair was mousy brown and cut into a classic bowl shape. He looked strange standing next to Percy, who himself was a slim, short, stylish, and slightly exotic looking. (Despite his claims of being Irish.) It was hard to imagine them knowing each other, much less being friends.

"Percy tells me you have an unwelcome guest in your bathroom," Nathan asked flatly.

"Yes, well, at least I hope it's still in the bathroom!" Chuck stated with the same look of horror he had outside the bathroom door.

Nathan walked over to the kitchen table and sat a green tote bag on its surface. He continued on to the bathroom door and opened it without hesitation. I didn't realize I was holding my breath until I felt a little dizzy. I slowly exhaled. I looked over at Chuck. He was pale and kept nervously rubbing his hands together. We could hear the shower door slide open. Nathan announced loudly to make sure we could hear him from the kitchen.

"Oh yeah, he's still in here. He's a big fella!"

He reentered the room and started rummaging through his tote bag. He pulled out a glass jar and a pair of disposable gloves, then went back into the bathroom. It wasn't but a second later that he emerged holding the jar, that now was filled with an ugly dark mass. Chuck squealed and ran to the far side of the room. He was performing a little hopping dance while shaking his arms as if the damn thing was clinging to him.

"Get it out of here! Take it outside and kill it!" His voice was shrill.

Nathan rose the glass jar to his face and looked at its contents carefully.

"It's a wolf spider. Spiders aren't bugs, you know. They're arachnids. I'll release him outside". With that, he placed the container back into the tote.

We all looked a bit aghast but managed to thank him profusely. Nathan left with the intruder. It took us a little while to regain composure.

Boyd finally jumped down from the fridge top. He landed on the counter, then bounded to the floor with a loud thud. He stretched, yawned, and sauntered over to his Tony the tiger food bowl. Apparently, it reminded Chuck that he, himself was hungry.

"What do you guys want for dinner?" He asked with enthusiasm.

Percy answered excitedly.

"Let's order pizza and breadsticks from Pizza Hut!"

"OK, that sounds good!" Chuck agreed through a beaming smile.

They both looked in my direction, hoping for an approval. I nodded my head in agreement.

I opened a can of chicken pate fancy feast and plopped it into the empty cat dish. I turned to Chuck.

"I told you spiders weren't bugs."

CHAPTER 15

LIQUOR'S QUICKER

For the last few days, I've been trying to overlook, as best I could, a throbbing toothache towards the back of my mouth. By Friday, it had gotten to be way too much to ignore. Knowing I wouldn't have another chance to call for an appointment until the next week, I decided to phone the dentist. I wasn't sure whether to be happy or bummed out about getting in as soon as Monday afternoon. The pain was horrible, but the thought of sitting in that chair was worse. I absolutely hate going to see that sadistic son of a bitch. I have never once walked out of his office without writhing in pain and feeling completely full of contempt. But at least I knew what to expect.

I pulled open the heavy glass door labeled Mark Spencer DDS. I stepped in and let it float slowly closed behind me. I walked up to the reception desk. Behind it in a chair was a sat a attractive blonde woman with a name tag that read Lacey.

She checked me in and told me to take a seat. I complied and pulled out my cell phone to text Chuck.

Me: Chuck, I'm at the dentist now. I finally came in to get my tooth taken care of. I'm not sure what he's going to do so I'm not sure how I'm gonna feel afterwards. If I'm totally screwed up, we might have to skip Monday night TV.

Chuck: Oh crap! That sucks, you better be OK! Good luck! Let me know when you're done.

Me: I will, thanks. I hit send and put my phone back into my pocket.

"The doctor will see you now." Lacey informed with a smile.

"Thank you," I replied as I walked past her and down the sterile hall of doom.

The door was open, so I walked in and sat on the orange plastic chair that looked like it came out of an elementary school cafeteria. I only had to wait about a minute before he bounded enthusiastically into the room. Doctor Spencer was an average-looking man, with a crew cut and a clean-shaven face. I would guess he was somewhere in his mid-40s. He's a very pleasant man, but because of his profession, I still don't like him.

"Well, good morning stranger, long time no see! You must be pretty desperate to pay me a visit! He exclaimed through a loud guffaw.

"Yah, that's about right." I winced and blinked nervously.

He laughed again and gestured me forward and patted the seat of "The Iron Chair." I stood up slowly and reluctantly climbed into it. My hands instantly squeezed the armrests, and I braced myself for the pending maltreatment.

I watched as he washed and gloved his hands and put on a disposable mask. He rolled his chair as close as he could, pushed up his sleeves, and reached for some sort of medieval dental device.

"OK, let's have a look at what's going on in there... open wide." He said a bit too eagerly.

He poked around, contorting my lips and cheeks with his tight-fitting rubber-gloved fingers.

"OK, I see we have a few issues. But we should be able to get you fixed up in just this one visit." With that, he rolled his chair back and peeled off his gloves.

"Rachel will be in to take X-rays and set up for us. I'll be back shortly." He informed and left the room.

I spent the next two hours white-knuckling the chair arms and bouncing the back of my heels on the footrest. Every muscle in my body was tense. I lay there with my eyes squeezed tightly shut, ashamed of my immaturity.

I walked down the sidewalk towards the bus stop. My mouth was so numb. I kept having to feel it to make sure the cotton I was supposed to be biting down on was still there. I felt like my face was drooping to one side, and I was pretty sure there was a bit of drooling going on. I sat on the bus, convinced that everyone was staring at me. I know the thought was ridiculous; I hoped it was ridiculous anyway.

I searched my pocket for my keys during my descent down the stairs to my basement apartment. When I got to the door, I realized I didn't need them. It was obvious that it wasn't locked because it was slightly ajar. My keys still in one hand, and the small bag the dentist gave me full of gauze and a new toothbrush in the other, I pushed it open with my forearm and went inside.

Chuck and Percy were in the kitchen, busying themselves with who knows what. I walked over to the dining room table and sat my stuff on it.

"Hey, what are you guys doing here?" I said through what felt like an extremely crooked and muted smile.

They both turned to me at the same time. Chuck had a sympathetic little grin. He cocked his head to one side and made a baby-like frown face.

"How are you doing? I never heard back from you, so I assumed we were still on for tonight. So here we are! Ready to smother you with the sympathy we know you were expecting!" He giggled and winked at Percy.

I slurred, "Fuck you" through the blood and saliva-saturated cotton. But I knew he was right.

I turned and headed for the bathroom. I grabbed the small bag the dentist gave me on my way in. I stood in front of the mirror and pulled the disgusting blob of gauze from my mouth. I was relieved that the bleeding had stopped, but I was still completely numb. I tossed the little bag into the cabinet under the sink. I looked back at myself in the mirror and tried to smile. No use. I left the bathroom in semi disgust and rejoined the girls in the kitchen.

Percy was leaning against the counter, watching Chuck pull tall water glasses from the cupboard. He set the glasses down beside two half-gallon jugs of alcohol, Grey goose vodka and cheap Monarch rum. He opened the freezer door and grabbed a box of sugar-free popsicles.

"What's it gonna be? We have orange, cherry, root beer,

or Dr. Pepper." He said inquisitively while holding the box in front of my face.

I'm assuming he read my expression and decided to explain.

"What flavor would you like? We're having popsicle dip cocktails. Pick a popsicle and a booze!" He prodded impatiently, giving the box a little shake.

"Vodka and orange!" I answered as quickly as possible through thick lips and tingling cheeks.

"I want rum and root beer!" Percy chimed in gleefully.

Chuck filled one of the glasses just shy of the rim with vodka. He unwrapped an orange pop and submerged it in the liquid. He handed it to me with a deviant grin.

"After a couple of these, you're going to want to make another dentist appointment!" He declared with giddy excitement and a squeal.

He turned to Percy with his palm in the air, and they executed an enthusiastic high 5. They laughed, and Percy jumped up and down while clapping his hands.

I looked down at the concoction I was holding. I was a little apprehensive when I pulled the wooden stick from the glass. I couldn't feel my lips yet, so I guess the whole thing was a little bit sloppy. I couldn't feel the juice as it ran over my chin, but I felt it when it landed on my chest. They stood and laughed hysterically as I continued trying my best to suck it, but I couldn't make my lips cooperate.

"Somebody could use some lessons!" Chuck joked and said in his thickest gay voice. I rolled my eyes.

With our drinks/dips in hand, we all congregated in the living room. Chuck had already adorned the couch with the clean floral sheet, so he and Percy assumed their regular positions. I sat in the armchair, as usual. Boyd was already straddled over the back; he made a good headrest.

Chuck turned on the television. He flipped through the channels, even though he knew we were going to set it on channel 66. Instead of the usual lineup programmed for Monday nights, this week was marathon week. Tonight, we would be watching back-to-back episodes of Bewitched.

"Bewitched night! Maybe we should watch TV tomorrow night too. It's going to be all I dream of Jeannie episodes!" Chuck gushed with way too much enthusiasm.

Not wanting to make a solid commitment at that moment, I told him we would have to play it by ear. I could tell he was a bit offended by my suggestion. He looked in my direction and shoved his entire root beer popsicle into his mouth. Then he preceded to demonstrate an animated version of fellatio. He pulled it slowly out of his mouth.

"That's the lesson you needed...." He said, smiling sarcastically.

"You're a real class act Chuck!" I said, trying unsuccessfully to hold back my laughter.

After about seven vodka-soaked popsicles, a traumatic assault on my oral cavity, and the wacky, flamboyant antics of two very gay gentlemen, I was ready to turn in for the evening. I stood up from my chair and stretched.

"I'm going to bed you guys. If you decide to stay over, be sure and lock the door."

"Already? We haven't even ordered a pizza yet!" Chuck said in amazement.

"First of all, I'm ready to drop on my ass, and second,

I probably couldn't chew it anyway. You guys enjoy. Good-night..."

I walked towards the kitchen. I rinsed my glass and filled it with cold water. I headed for my bedroom and performed my nightly routine before slipping under the covers. I always slept with the door open wide enough for Boyd to come and go freely.

Despite being exhausted and more than a little drunk, sleep didn't come easily. I just laid there and listened to the "girls" banter and giggle out in the living room. They talked about the usual stuff they discussed when I wasn't around. They learned quickly what subjects to avoid in my presence. I think they got tired of hearing my same old smart-ass remarks.

I was close to drifting off when something about their conversation changed. It caught my attention, and my ears perked up. I'm pretty sure they thought I was asleep.

"Have you heard back from the doctor yet?" Percy said a little louder than he should have.

Chuck didn't reply. They were quiet for a minute, so I assumed Chuck had shushed him. He wasn't absolutely positive I was asleep. This was a story he didn't want me to hear, at least not yet.

CHAPTER 16

The Jigs Up

I didn't normally feel this shitty on a Tuesday morning. It was after 9:00 AM, and Boyd wanted his breakfast. He woke me up by pressing a baseball-mitt-sized paw against various areas of my face. The hard push to my eyeball is what finally snapped me out of my coma.

"OK, OK fatty! Geez!" I scolded him despite my sore jaw.

The numbness from the lidocaine shot was long gone. And at that moment, I was certainly missing it. I cradled my cheek in my palm, which made sitting up to get out of bed even more difficult. My feet finally planted on the floor, I debated on proceeding. As I sat on the edge, I let my mind replay the previous evening. It made me smile. Why does having a good time with my friends have to come at a cost all the time? I knew damn well why. We associate fun with alcohol. The thought made me chuckle quietly. I got up slowly and headed toward the bathroom. I reached in and flicked the light on. At that very same moment, I remembered Percy asking Chuck a question. He wanted to know if he had heard back from the doctor.

My apartment only has one bathroom. It has a door that opens to the living room and one that opens into my bedroom. More than likely, an idea of some frugal architect... a way to add an ensuite at very little cost. I took care of my morning business and hesitantly peeked out the bathroom door into the living room. I wasn't happy at the view, but I entered it anyway.

Chuck was sprawled out on the Big L in his usual drunken "morning after" position. His mouth was gaped open, and the plump arm that wouldn't fit on the couch with him draped to the floor.

Percy was in a fetal position in front of the television, snoring lightly and clutching the ugly brown and orange Afghan my mother gave me when I moved out. A little miffed, I stood and surveyed the mess. It was obvious what they did after I went to sleep. A large pizza box holding crust edges only. An uneaten slice was lying face down on the floor by the coffee table. There were multiple popsicle wrappers, popcorn kernels, and various potato chip bags strewn about. I walked over to the front door to see if they had locked it like I had told them to. I grabbed the knob. Not only did they not lock it, but they didn't even make sure it was shut. I thought about waking them up and kicking some ass. Instead, I decided to go for a walk and get a bit of fresh air. I left my very large and very hungry cat to take care of their punishment.

I had decided to buy a newspaper and head for McDonald's. I ordered a large black coffee and a sausage McMuffin with egg and cheese. I slid across the smoothly crafted orange Mcbench of a corner booth and settled in for some alone time.

I needed to think about how I was going to approach Chuck about his Doctor secret. It was obviously something he didn't want to share with me. I wasn't sure whether to be offended that he felt he couldn't confide in me or pissed that he shared whatever it was with Percy. It was two hours later that I arrived home. I had to use my key to get in, that meant some sort of action took place in my absence. The mess had been cleaned up, Boyd had been fed, and the apartment was empty. In an instant, all had been forgiven.

It wasn't till about 4:00 o'clock that afternoon that I felt ready to confront Chuck. I had gone over a dozen or more scenarios in my head over the course of the day about how to broach the subject. None of them seemed right, so I discarded them as stupid ideas. I was just going to go up to his apartment and ask him straight out what was going on. Kind of like ripping off a band-aid.

I slowly climbed the stairs to his apartment and hesitated for a moment at the top. Then I just went for it.

Knock, knock... I wasn't sure why I knocked. I always did. When he came to my place, he adopted the open-door policy on his own volition and just barged in.

I stood and listened for footsteps. But instead, heard a voice from within.

"Come in!" He chimed loudly.

I opened the door wide enough to stick my head in.

"It's me...." I called out as I came the rest of the way in.

I walked over to the muted red velvet couch. It always

reminded me of something you would find in France a couple hundred years ago. It was tufted with velvet-covered buttons and had scuffed up wooden claw feet, that he vows to restore soon.

"What's up?" He inquired from within the bathroom.

"I was wondering if you had a few minutes to chat?"

"Do you wanna come in here? You can sit on the toilet lid and talk while I put my face on." He suggested with an air of insistence.

OK..." I answered and hoisted myself up.

I entered the bathroom and slid myself around his protruding butt, and made my way to the toilet seat... but opted for the edge of the tub. There was a puffy neon pink rug hanging over its edge that looked more comfortable.

He turned in my direction and leaned his hip against the vanity for support.

"So, what did you wanna talk about? I hope you're not mad. We cleaned up good before we left. I fed Boyd and gave him fresh water!"

"NO! No, nothing like that, and thank you for doing it." My words stammered a little as I spoke. His eyebrows furrowed as he looked at me questioningly.

"Then what's going on?" He asked with suspicion.

"Last night when I was lying in bed, I heard Percy ask you if you had heard from the doctor. I was wondering what that was all about. Are you OK? What doctor and what's going on?"

There. I asked him. It wasn't that hard. I'm not sure what I was so worried about?

"Oh that. I was hoping you hadn't heard him." He said

with a tinge of disappointment, then turned back to the mirror and picked up his eyebrow pencil.

"I'll call Percy and tell him I'm going to be a little late."

I sat and watched him finish putting on his face. He didn't speak again until he was sure he looked just right. He replaced the cap on a lipstick tube and opened the top bathroom drawer. In one fell swoop of a forearm, all of the makeup went inside, and he shut it. He looked over at me while rubbing his lips together, making sure the application was spread evenly.

"Let's sit at the table. I'll make us a drink, and we can talk." He said as he made his exit. He gestured me to follow with a wave of his hand. I stood and followed behind him. When I reached the table, I pulled out a chair and sat down. I watched him prepare the libations. He looked perfectly relaxed. He put a straw in each glass, swiveled their contents, and delivered them to the table. He took a seat and a large swig of his vodka and Diet Coke. He pulled his cell phone out from his breast pocket and swiped at the screen. Before placing his call, he took a moment to burp into his fist.

"Hi doll! Look, I'm going to be a little late, so I'll just meet you there." He paused for a moment and listened. "No, everything is fine. I won't be long. See you there." He pressed the end button and returned the phone to his pocket.

He lifted his drink and placed his elbows on the table. A wide toothy smile appeared on his face.

"let's talk." He suggested through the smile.

CHAPTER 17

THE EXPLANATION

I sat opposite from him at the table and waited patiently. He still had a strange smile on his face, his eyes on mine. If I didn't know better, I'd have thought he was enjoying the procrastination as much as his cocktail. He took another large swig and noticed he had emptied his glass.

"Oh my! Looks like I need a refill!" He grabbed the table and pushed his chair backwards. "How about you? Care for a refill?" Smile still wide, he stood, burped, and waited for my reply.

"Sure, why not! Seems we suddenly have all the time in the world!" I announced loudly through a thick accent of sarcasm. I held out my glass of ice in his direction. He took it from me and made a flamboyant spin before heading into the kitchen.

"Here you go, Doll!" He chimed as he handed my now full glass back to me. He repositioned himself in his chair. Before setting his drink back down, he grabbed a napkin from the holder in the middle of the table and wiped up a puddle of condensation. I knew he was stalling when he jumped up and went into the living room.

"Chuck!? What the fuck are you doing now!?" I demanded. My patience was wearing pretty thin by that point.

He came around the corner from the living room, waving a stack of coasters from the coffee table.

"Will you just sit the fuck down!"

"OK! OK!" He practically yelped as he landed heavily back in his seat.

"Come on Chuck, no more screwing around. What's going on?" I asked him in a calm voice. "You know you can tell me anything. What's the big secret?" I sat and waited for him to collect his thoughts and decide on his presentation.

He continued sipping on his drink. He avoided my stare, but I could see the thoughtful look on his face. He fiddled with the damp napkin. I sat patiently. He finally looked up at me and pulled in a breath, the way you do when you're ready to speak.

"I'm currently in the market for a new dick." He blurted. He sat practically frozen with his eyes locked on mine. I could tell he was waiting for my reaction. Frankly, so was I. What the hell do you say after an announcement like that? I took a long swig of my vodka and 7UP. I guess I was the one procrastinating now.

"What?" Yep, that's what I came up with. I sat and stared at him several seconds more before I continued. "You're in the market for a dick?!... What exactly does that mean? You're in the market for a dick? Is there a dick market?!" As the words flew out of my mouth hysterically, I realized I needed to get ahold of myself and let him explain.

"I've been working with doctors here and in Seattle. I've had several interviews and tests. I've been approved for a transplant, and I'm waiting for a donor. I'm sure you have a million questions!" He rambled the words as fast as he could say them, undoubtedly, to keep me from interrupting before he could finish.

"OK, you're right. I do have a million questions!" I instantly felt kind of bad about the way I said it. I didn't sound like the kind of person you could tell anything to.

"I knew this day was coming, and I prepared a paper for you to read. I'm going to go upstairs and get it for you now. That way you will have a much better idea of what I'm talking about. Maybe you will calm down a bit and act at least somewhat rationally." With that, Chuck stood and swigged the rest of his beverage. He replaced the glass on the table and said, "I'll be back in a second." I kept my mouth shut because I could tell he was in a no-nonsense mood. I watched him head for the door. He left without looking back.

I sat there alone at the table, full of remorse. I always say that I'm understanding and a good friend. But when it comes down to proving it, I seem to come up short. Don't get me wrong. I mean it when I say it. I just have a problem with the way I handle surprises. I really need to work on that.

I didn't even know I was hunched over until I heard the door reopen. The sound of it made me spontaneously sit up in full attention. Percy walked in and shut it behind him. I felt myself slouch again. He looked around the room with a questioning face.

"Hi, is Chuck down here?"

"He ran upstairs for something; he'll be back in a second. Have a seat." He headed straight for the kitchen and mixed himself a drink. He had barely sat down when Chuck reentered the apartment. He walked towards me, holding a single piece of typing paper. He gave it to me and headed back around the table to take his seat. He looked at Percy and smiled.

"I thought I might find you here. You were taking so long. I got tired of waiting, so I decided to head over and just meet you here. Hope I'm not interrupting? Everything OK?" Percy said nervously, looking back and forth between us. You could see that he was questioning his decision to just pop in.

"Drink up Love. We need to get going." Chuck informed affectionately with a wink.

Percy preceded to down his rum and root beer in one smooth gulp. He stood and let out a gasp of refreshment, licked his lips, and carried his glass to the sink.

I sat looking at the typed paper without actually reading. I would wait for the two of them to leave. I watched as they headed toward the door and slipped on their coats. Before leaving, Chuck turned around and put a hand up in a small wave.

"I'll call you when I get home tonight."

He smiled and shut the door behind him.

I decided to move into the living room. I picked up my drink and reading material, then made my way to the Big L. I clicked on the table lamp. I realized all the coasters were in the dining room. I made my way back over to the table and restacked the stamped-out cork circles. Why did he have to move them all? There were only two of us at the table... why did he have to bring all six? I shook my head and laughed to myself. Because Chuck, is Chuck.

I had some reading to do. I picked up the document and read it carefully. About a minute and a half later, I felt I had a full understanding of Chuck's situation.

Anticipated penis transplant questions. By Chuck Barnes

Q. Where do you get a penis for a transplant?

1. The families of deceased donors. There are organizations that take care of the arrangements for them.

Q. How do you know if you're eligible for a new penis?

1. You have to go through testing. Your donor must have the same blood and tissue types and skin color blah blah blah. Then you go on a list and wait.

Q. When will you have the transplant?

1. You can get called in for surgery at any time as soon as a donor becomes available. So, you better be ready to go lickety split.

Q. How long will it take?

1. They say you can expect to be in the hospital from four weeks to three months or so. it depends on different things, like how much help you have at home, how far away you live from the hospital, and stuff like that.

Q. When it's all said and done what can you expect?

1. To be able to pee standing up, and to have sex. And take anti-rejection drugs so it doesn't fall off.

Q. How much is this going to cost!?

1. Approximately 16 to $19,000 dollars.

Q. Where is the money coming from?

1. That's where you come in.

It all became crystal clear as to why he didn't want to tell me about this right away.

I heard the muted ruckus that occurs when Chuck arrives home late at night. I picked up my phone from the nightstand to check the time. 2:15 AM. I hoped he knew better than to call me this late. I waited and listened to the footsteps above me. They didn't last long. He must have decided to turn in. Good boy. I knew I wouldn't hear from him until later the next day.

You know how your voice sounds when you're startled out of a dead sleep to answer the phone? That's how Chuck's voice sounded when I called him at 3:15 in the afternoon the next day.

"Hello."

"Why the fuck are you still in bed?" I demanded in disgust.

"I didn't get to sleep till about 2:30 this morning!" He whined.

"Ah geez! So sorry to disturb you after only 13 hours of sleep! Get up, you lazy fat ass; we need to go to the store. There's absolutely no food down here, for people or cats. And more importantly, the booze supply's getting dangerously low!" I admit my presentation was a bit exaggerated. I heard him groan.

"Let me take a shower first. I'll come down." Then he hung up on me.

45 minutes later, the door opened. He didn't come in; he just yelled.

"Come on, let's go, Chop chop!" He slapped the door with his open fist to coincide with his chops.

I could tell it surprised him when I came around the corner wearing my coat. I was ready to go, and it annoyed him.

"Yes Sir, let's hit the road!" I sang cheerfully. Man, if looks could kill…

We walked the few blocks to Safeway and discussed the fun he and Percy had the previous evening. As we talked, I was hoping for an opening in the conversation that I could interject the transplant subject into. Chuck rambled on about how delicious the food was, how drunk they got, and all the people they ran into. I was convinced he was avoiding the subject. I decided to let it go until he was ready. I would wait until he brought it up.

As we entered the parking lot of the store, Chuck pulled a cart from the return corral. Its loose wheels spun in circles and dragged across the bumpy pavement. The unmistakable, gravely rattling sound it made stopped when we reached the black mat that opens the glass double doors leading into the building.

We stepped inside and were at once greeted by a huge display of Cheetos.

"2 for 6!" Chuck absolutely loves Cheetos and grabbed two family-sized bags. One of each variety, a crunchy and a puffy.

"Take it easy Chuck... we gotta haul all this shit home." I reminded him.

"Oh fooey!" He dismissed me with a flick of his wrist.

"We can get an Uber if we buy too much stuff. Come on."

And off he went down aisle 1, I followed. We grabbed a 7-pound bag of cat food, 12 cans of fancy feast pate, a six-pack of toilet paper, and two half gallons of booze. After those were in the cart, I lost interest in shopping. Chuck, on the other hand, was just getting started.

We went down every single aisle, some twice. Chuck made it a rule to go down the freezer aisle and the deli aisle last. It ensured that everything would stay cold for the trip home. We strolled down the freezer aisle to the ice cream case. Two pints of butter pecan, two boxes of sugar-free popsicles, and we were ready for the deli.

Individually wrapped American cheese, check. 16-ounce tub of low-fat cottage cheese, check. One pound block of salted butter, check. One pound package of Oscar Mayer bologna, check.... Then it happened; the hot dog section.

"Oh my." He stood with one hand on his hip and the other gripping the handle of the cart, staring down at the selection of wieners.

"Don't worry Chuck. I got you covered buddy." I told him. He reached a plump arm around my shoulders and pulled me next to him in a playful hug...

"Stop it, Chuck." I teased. "I'll call the Uber."

CHAPTER 18

WALTER BROWER

Once again, I found myself pulling open the large glass doors that led to the interior of Blushing Meadows. And like every other Sunday before this one, I stated on cue.

"I can't believe it's already been a week. I feel like I'm constantly walking through that fucking door."

I felt Chuck pat me on the back reassuringly as he passed me on his way to the front desk.

"Good morning, Marianne!" He chimed, just like he had the week before, and the week before that. And in turn, Marianne Ignored him as usual.

We went about the usual crap, and as usual, the day dragged on about as fast as a slug nailed to the floor. Everything went like slow clockwork. Nothing out of the ordinary, which was good. This is one place you don't want to be surprised. We were on the last hour of our volunteer day when Chuck reminded me that we would be visiting Walter Brower instead of Carole Stapleton.

We stood outside the door of room 111. We just stood there. After a few moments, Chuck turned to me and said through a sigh. "I guess one of us should knock." Then we stood there a few more minutes. It startled me when he suddenly used the side of his fist to bang on the door a couple times.

"Hello? Mr. Brower?" Chuck cooed cheerfully and loudly enough to penetrate through the wooden door. We stood and listened... nothing.

"Mr. Brower? Are you in there? We are here to visit you for a while." He tried again, smiling at me as he spoke. Still nothing.

I stepped back a bit and suggested quietly that maybe we lucked out and the old bastard was dead. Chuck rolled his eyes at me and gave the door another couple whacks.

"I'm just gonna go in." He informed me as he turned the knob. He gave a slight push, and the door swung open. He glanced back at me before making a confident entrance into Walter's domain. He walked directly across the room towards the little old man sitting in a chair at a desk by the window.

"Good afternoon, Walter!" Chuck said in a loud friendly tone. "We've come to brighten your day, by spending the next hour keeping you company and getting to know each other!"

"Get the hell out of my room!" Walter demanded as he reached around the back of his chair and grabbed his cane.

Chuck's hands flew up in the air, and he quickly stepped backward several feet.

"Whoa, whoa! Walter! Take it easy man. We're just here to visit, thought you might like some company today!" He pleaded apologetically.

"Well, you thought wrong, you fat fairy! Now get out before my cane shows you who's boss!" He fired at Chuck. His face turning bright red, accentuating his rosacea.

I couldn't help it. I started laughing. I couldn't stop. The look on Chuck's face was priceless. A mixture of disbelief, shock, and surprise... all wrapped up in a huge smile. He burst out laughing as he ran back toward me and the door. He squealed and grabbed my shoulders and pushed me back into the hallway, as carefully and as quickly as possible, then closed the door behind us. Neither of us could get a hold of ourselves. We stood and laughed, occasionally grabbing our stomachs, and giving each other playful shoves.

Marianne's shrill voice cut through the guffaws like a sharp knife. We at once snapped to attention.

"What's going on down here!?" She roared, as she charged towards us down the hallway like a rogue rhinoceros. "There are patients trying to sleep in this wing!" She stood in front of us, her hands planted firmly on her hips, scolding loudly.

Chuck, normally the conformist in any situation, decided on a different route that afternoon. I'm not sure what got into him, but I thoroughly enjoyed the performance that ensued,

"Oh, for God's sake Marianne! A bullhorn couldn't wake these deaf old farts!" He blasted through a taunting snicker. Then he started twisting his hips and jumping up and down while simulating fart noises through his pursed lips. I stood and watched him. I was both stunned and thrilled at the sight of him. There was no controlling my hysterical laughter.

Marianne was far from amused. Her face twisted in anger and her fists curled tightly by her sides. We could see her tremble as she screamed. "QUIET!"

Of course, this only made us laugh harder, if that was possible. Suddenly Chuck started skipping in a very exaggerated way towards the exit. My eyes widened, and my laughter stopped momentarily as I realized he was leaving me alone with Marianne. I ran after him. When I caught up, he was pushing the glass door open. I flew past him and down the cement steps, leading to freedom... forever for me, until next Sunday for Chuck.

CHAPTER 19

NO FAVORS

"I told Chuck I would pay for his operation," I informed Doctor Kelley enthusiastically. "I'm so grateful I'm in a position to help him like this!"

The expression on her face turned skeptical. She raised her pointer finger and tsked me. Of course, it pissed me off. Instantly on the defensive, I kept my cool and let her talk.

"I understand you wanting to help out your friend and how he would take precedence over money...."

I had to stop her right there. I didn't like where this was going or the vibe I was getting. I put a hand up to halt her. She complied. She understood Chuck was important to me and took precedence over money?! Well, no shit, glad to know you've been listening! I felt the heat rise in my cheeks. I needed to rein myself in.

I hate when someone tries to tell me how I think and feel. I guess that may sound a bit strange coming from someone that spends so much time in a shrink's office, voluntarily, no less.

We decided (she decided) that we would spend today's session discussing the role money plays in my personal relationships. She asked if there were many, if any, instances where individuals targeted me for my money. Did they ever just treat me like a dollar sign? Was she fucking kidding? Of course! But those were the assholes I made the mistake of telling I had money. Anyone that just meets me sees where I live and the caliber of people I hang with would assume I'm penniless.

She commented that even if I didn't initially reveal my good fortune, it would surely surface eventually. I assured her that the people who were around long enough to be told had earned my trust by then. She seemed satisfied with that answer. I tried to convince her there were certain people who need only to ask for help and aren't questioned, like Chuck. Then there were the "no way in hell" folks, like my brothers. Finally, there is the "maybe, depending on what it's for" category. This is where "the couple" fits in.

* * *

I was half asleep on the Big L about 8:00 on a Wednesday night. I could hear Boyd snoring lightly on the armrest behind my head. We were both startled when the phone rang. He bolted for the bedroom. I'm always amazed at how fast he can run, despite how fat he is. I rolled over and grabbed my phone off of the coffee table, and checked the screen to see who was so rudely interrupting us. It was Jerry. I groaned and put the phone back down, waiting to see if he would leave a message. He did.

"Hey stranger! This is Jerry, of Donna and Jerry. How

ya do 'in? You came up in a conversation last night, and we decided to give you a jingle." He left his number, requested a return phone call, and hung up.

I saved the message just in case I decided to call him back. I turned off my phone and headed for bed. It was early, but I didn't care. I was dead tired. Boyd was curled up fast asleep on the pillow next to mine. I lay down beside him and quickly found myself drifting off, but not before I decided I would call Jerry back tomorrow. I didn't think I could live the rest of my life wondering what the hell they wanted, and how they were going to try and drag me into it.

I woke up unusually early, no surprise, since I was asleep before most kindergarteners have dinner. Fuzznuts was still snoring beside me, and probably would be for many hours to come. I was a little dizzy when I stood up out of bed, probably from sleeping so long. I headed directly for the shower and checked for spiders before stepping in. I may need to bring this new phobia to doctor Kelley's attention. I treated myself to a 10-minute hot shower and loved every second of it. As I was toweling off, I remembered my pending call to Jerry.

"Hello!" Donna's voice rang in my ear. She obviously recognized my number.

"Hi Donna, is Jerry around? I'm returning his call."

"Yes, I'll get him for you!" She sounded anxious to put him on the phone.

Jerry took the phone and was quick to invite me, Chuck, and Percy to a dinner party, planned for Friday night around 7:00 o'clock. Not unlike Chuck, I find it hard to say no to free food and drinks. I accepted his invitation on behalf of the three of us. I pretended to think it was just a gathering of people. A gathering for no other reason than fun, food, booze, and bullshiting. But of course, I knew that wasn't the case. People in my position don't experience such simple happenings. My invitations are usually from opportunists, looking for some sort of monetary help. This one turned out to be no exception.

Chuck was giddy with excitement the whole drive over to Donna and Jerry's. He was definitely a party guy. Percy and I exchanged wide-eyed looks when Chuck started singing, "It's my party and I'll cry if I want to" in one of the most ridiculously animated voices ever. We laughed our way up to their front door. I knocked loudly.

The door swung open and revealed a beaming Jerry.

"Hello! Welcome, please come in!" He said as he stepped back, swinging his arm to gesture the way.

The three of us entered the foyer, and Jerry closed the door. He led us through the beautiful house to the amazing gourmet kitchen. Donna looked over at us from the sink. She quickly dried her hands, threw down the dishtowel and made a beeline in our direction.

"Hello, you three! It's so good to see you again. Welcome to our home!" She gushed as she pulled us in for a group hug.

Chuck was beaming, Percy wore a polite smile, and I was looking forward to finding out the reason we were there.

We were led out to the pool and patio area. There were other guests, all sitting, sipping drinks, and chatting.

Donna and Jerry's place was amazing. Maybe I was wrong, maybe this was a friendly invitation only. They appeared to be quite well off. I decided to relax and enjoy their hospitality.

Chuck and Percy each got a cocktail and immediately

removed their footwear. They spent most of the evening with their feet dangling in the warm pool water. I chatted with some folks (looking back, they may have been just props.) I drank several icy cold import beers and ate about 30 of the most succulent jumbo shrimp I had ever tasted. I was having a great time and had let my guard down. That's when they made their move.

As if on cue, they rallied around me. They pulled their resin patio chairs as close as they possibly could to ensure that I had no route of escape. I was trapped. My body tensed up and I felt a surge of dread. I looked across the pool at Chuck, sending one of those "help me" looks. He smiled and waved, he was either too far away to notice my expression, or he decided to ignore it. We would be having a chat about it later.

I sat there, wide-eyed, scanning their faces. I was churning excuses in my mind to decline any request they threw at me before even hearing the proposal. I felt kind of proud of myself. I realized I was one of very few people that could drink heavily and still use the word "no."

Jerry nervously cleared his throat.

"How have you been doing lately?" He asked.

It was obviously rhetorical. You would have thought he could have come up with something better. At least something he hadn't already asked me before. Donna was seated next to him with a large plastered on smile, and it seemed as if she had forgotten how to blink.

"What's going on here?" I asked suspiciously.

He sat silent for a few seconds before confessing that he had a proposition. I forced back a sarcastic quip. He assured me it was a sound plan and a solid money-making opportunity. I reminded him that I already had money. He ignored me and continued.

He looked down at his hands, each tenaciously clinging to a boney knee. He took a deep breath, exhaled slowly, and lifted his eyes to mine.

"First, I would like to ask you to listen quietly to our proposal. Please don't interject until I am completely finished. OK?" He practically begged.

I nodded in agreement. I was enjoying his nervousness. I could sense that I was the key to the plan, whatever it might be. Ah, the power.

Apparently, Jerry and Donna had a newfound interest. It started as a hobby. They quickly found out, coincidentally, that their newfound leisure activity could be a big money-making opportunity. Problem is, with new ventures comes a need for startup capital. That's where I came in. Upon listening to his following story, I decided to pass on his so-called investment opportunity.

I didn't think funding underground porn was what my grandparents had in mind for their life savings. Well, maybe grandpa wouldn't have minded, but still.

Jerry explained that he had set up a camera in his and Donna's bedroom. That alone was far too much detail for me. He claimed his intention was to produce an erotic video for the two of them to enjoy and share with friends. Now mind you, this story from any other couple would have made me a bit uncomfortable. But hearing crap like this from these two felt as normal as taking a dump.

They began their cinematic masterpiece with an elaborate fight scene. It's filled with copious sobbing, screaming, and face slapping. Of course, this all leads to apologies, hugging and kissing. And as you can imagine, the rest of the film consists of things you would certainly never want to see your friends doing together. (Ones from any category) Supposedly, the mini-movie ends with the predictable clinking of champagne glasses and profuse cigarette smoking.

Apparently, a few weeks after they wrapped their production, they had a party. Just the right combination of alcohol and people, led to their debut screening. They received 5-star reviews and requests for more material.

I was unaware of it at the time, but Jerry had lost his job. He and Donna suddenly found themselves living beyond their means. I guess they thought becoming movie producers was the answer to all their problems. And who better to ask for funding than someone in the "just a step above acquaintance" category that you hadn't even spoke to in over a year?

CHAPTER 20

A GATE OPENS

I walked in the creepy old office building at five minutes to 3:00, checked in with Teresa at the desk, then headed into Doctor Kelley's office. After making sure that there was ample vanilla creamer, I brewed a cup of coffee and took a seat on my end of the hard-ass new couch I hated so much.

I didn't want to be there. I wanted to be laying on the big L with Boyd, watching TV and enjoying a Starbucks mocha with a small squirt of caramel and a big blob of whipped cream. I told myself to try and make today's session as brief as possible. Trouble is I talk too much. While trying to say very little, I end up blabbing my way into a full-blown discussion on all the crap I wanted to avoid. For instance, if Dr. Kelley says something I don't completely agree with, I argue instead of letting it go. Why can't I ever just call and say I won't be in? Maybe it's because she charges a fee for missed appointments?... Am I really that stinking cheap? Chronic frugality; another reason I should probably be here.

At 10 minutes after 4:00, Doctor Kelley hurried through the door.

"I'm so sorry I'm late!" She sounded winded as she apologized. "I ran into a colleague I needed to discuss something with in the lobby." With that, she rolled back her oversized office chair and plopped down heavily, then scooted herself up against the cluttered desk. Her tardiness made me wonder if she prorated my bill in cases like these. Oh yeah, I'm cheap.

"So, how was your week? Any exciting new adventures?" She asked, almost in jest.

I told her that Chuck, Percy, and I went to a cocktail party at Donna and Jerry's house. She raised her eyebrows in interest.

I described their big, beautiful home with the luxury swimming pool. I told her how delicious the shrimp was and that they had an outdoor bar full of any and all libations. I also told her my suspicions had been correct, that I was invited there for a specific reason. I described the proposal they presented me with. I could tell she was enjoying the story. She listened quietly with slight smile on her lips, and her eyes practically twinkled as if she were hearing some really juicy gossip. I added a few made-up and completely unnecessary details, solely designed to enhance the story for her pleasure. I rarely have someone so riveted.

When my account finally concluded, I could see by her facial expression that she was switching to her questioning mode. It was at that point I resolved to the fact that we were going to be here for a full session. I decided to concede and relax.

As if she wanted me to make a confession, her eyes squinted slightly, and she leaned forward as she asked me a question.

"Did you accept their hospitality knowing full well that no matter what they asked, your answer was going to be no?"

"Yes, I suppose I did!" I confessed through a beaming smile. I suddenly assumed a mock sober face before quickly adding, "Unless of course it was some sort of medical emergency, then I would have certainly helped. Like for instance, if Jerry needed an emergency ass enhancement!"

She assumed a sarcastic smile. So much for my attempt at humor.

For some reason, she always brought up my finances. She couldn't seem to grasp my categories theory. I didn't feel like explaining it again but tried to put it in a nutshell for her. I may have come off as a little impatient.

"Look, Chuck is my best friend. Donna and Jerry have dropped from the "just above acquaintances" category to the just "acquaintances" category. I really don't understand your confusion?"

She smiled and offered an understanding nod. We only had a few moments left in the session, so I thought that would be it for the day. Wrong again.

"What would you do if a family member asked you for money? Would it depend on what they wanted it for, or would you provide it, regardless of the reason?"

Was she joking? I told her it would depend on which family member, and yes, it would depend on what they needed it for.

Thank God our time was up for that afternoon.

Unfortunately, she had managed to open a door in my mind before I could escape. Randy and Troy had been let loose.

CHAPTER 21

MY CHILDHOOD IN A NUTSHELL

My mom and dad were pretty cool. So, it seemed at the time. They provided us with all of the best, maybe beyond. We had a nice house. Each of us kids had our own bedroom, decorated just the way we liked it. The basement was finished and was full of the usual stuff a group of spoiled kids would have. There was a pool table, TV, stereo, and assorted beanbag chairs along with the couch and loveseat. Out in the garage were all kinds of sporting equipment and bicycles. The backyard was fenced. It was perfect for game playing and birthday parties. To the unknowing eye, it looked as if we had a perfect childhood. In actuality for my sister and me, it was more like a nightmare.

I grew up the third child out of four. My two older brothers, Randy, and Troy were what most people would describe as spawn of the devil himself. My younger sister, Joy, on the other hand, was nothing short of an angel. She was a dainty little child, looked frail, and had an innocence written on her cherubic face. She was the kind of kid you felt oddly sorry for, purely because of her appearance. Intellectually however, she was a giant. I never felt that my need to protect her and watch out for her was anything more than a physical necessity.

Unbeknownst to our parents, Randy and Troy had complete control of our household. Joy and I were completely manipulated by them. Ruled by fear and iron fists, which were oblivious to our mom and dad. Randy was the oldest and was a power step above Troy. We were aware of their status, but we were equally afraid of them both. It didn't matter who thumped you, it hurt just the same.

Every day began the same for my sister and me. A sucker punch to the side or top of the head was our alarm clock. Both of our parents worked and left the house very early. They left it up to Randy to guide the rest of us through the morning, and out the door to school. I gotta tell ya, those were some pretty scary and eventful mornings, downright torturous. There was plenty of teasing, punching, kicking, screaming, and crying. I think Joy and I could have possibly been the only two kids in the world that actually looked forward to spending the whole day at school. It was our safe haven.

After school wasn't quite as bad for us as before school. We could usually avoid our brothers on the walk home. We knew that if we screwed around long enough on the way there, our folks might be back from work when we finally arrived. The two of them being home, made it difficult for the dickheads to torture us.

I look back at those days now and find it hard to believe our parents were so oblivious. How could they not know what was going on in their absence? Were they so self-absorbed that we came off as just things living in their home? Granted, they weren't there much, but for God's sake, we had scars! I also realize now how we should have been honest with them; we should have let them know the torture we were enduring. But at the time, we believed if we told on our older brothers, they would exact a raging revenge. Had I known then what I know now, I would have blown the whistle on them. Short of killing us, it really couldn't have gotten much worse.

There were two different routes from our house to school. Joy and I tried hard to make sure we chose the opposite of Troy and Randy's route. Most days it was easy to avoid them. They would usually hang out with the other fucked up malevolent bastards that went to our school. They would all stand around smoking cigarettes and plotting their evil. We would just watch them until they picked a path home. And voila, we knew which route to take. But there were days that we weren't so lucky.

We were walking side by side, at a sluggish pace, I was looking down at my feet over the thick stack of books I had pressed against my chest. My left shoe was untied. I was almost mesmerized by the laces as they flopped around my shoe, threatening to trip me. It was a large pile of dog poop that snapped me out of my trance. I stepped around it. I was happy to have dodged that bullet.

"Hang on Joy," I told her as I knelt down to tie it.

"No!" I heard her suddenly scream.

I felt the bottom of a cowboy boot slam into the center of my back. The sheer force of the kick knocked the wind out of me. My forehead made a disturbingly loud thud when it smacked the dirt path beneath it. My arms were still wrapped around the books, now also pinned to the ground. I couldn't breathe or move. I was afraid of what they would do to Joy.

After what seemed an eternity, I was able to turn my head in her direction. My eyes met her pink tennis shoes as they were backing up, away from Troy's advancement.

"Leave us alone!" I heard her beg desperately. Her plea was met with laughter, and a much too powerful shove to the face that sent her to a brutal landing on her back.

I struggled to pull my arms out from beneath me. My ears were ringing, but I could still hear the taunts and laughter. I finally managed to roll onto my side and pushed myself up into a sitting position. Joy was a couple feet away, sobbing and clutching her nose. Her face and hands were quickly turning red. Shoving my books out of the way, I crawled to my bleeding baby sister as fast as my weakness would allow. I reached around her head and pulled her sweatshirt hood to her gushing nose. I glared up at the two most vile assholes alive. They just stood there grinning at us, arms folded across their puffed-up chests.

To this day, I have never felt rage the way I did at that moment. I was well aware that if I were to lip off at them or show any sign of intent to fight back, my life could be dramatically shortened. I decided to risk it, who the hell wanted to live like that anyway?

Joy and I remained huddled on the ground together. I decided to sit and wait, to see what they had planned for us next. I knew, foolishly, that I wasn't going to take whatever it was lying down, at first anyway.

It seemed they were satisfied with their work. Randy gave Troy one of those congratulatory slaps on the back.

"Let's head home man, I think these two dumbshits have had enough for today, at least till we get home!" He said through a sinister laugh.

"Yeah, I suppose, I could use a sandwich anyway," Troy added before starting home.

On their way past us, Randy decided to give my thigh a bonus kick. I saw Troy behind him getting ready to do the same. I waited for the perfect second and stuck my leg out in front of him, he fell hard and fast. Because he didn't have time to catch himself, he landed flat on his face. Randy spun around and grabbed him by his shirt and pulled him to his feet. I felt completely elated. I didn't even care that it was quite possibly the last thing I would ever do.

I could see Troy fighting back tears. His nose was bleeding hard. I couldn't have been happier to see it.

"Now you're gonna die!" Troy said as he examined his blood-soaked hand.

"How do you think we should handle this one Troy?" Randy asked, smiling from ear to ear.

Troy wiped his hand slowly down his side as he glared into my eyes. The satisfaction I was feeling turned quickly to horror.

"Get up you little stupid motherfucker!"

I let out a terrified stream and grabbed for his hand as he pulled me to my feet by my hair. My feet were almost off the ground when he punched me in the stomach as hard as he could. Immediately after the blow he let go of my hair and

I feel to the ground in a rumpled pile. Once again, I found myself breathless and unable to move. I could only watch as Randy dragged Joy by her blood-soaked hoodie up the path. Her screams rang in my ears. It was torture not being able to help. Unbeknownst to me at the time, I would experience that horrible feeling again someday.

Troy walked past me towards his mentor, but not before kicking another blast of dirt into my face.

"Hurry up man, you're gonna wanna see this!" Randy yelled back to him in excitement.

Troy's pace quickened. Upon his arrival, they both started laughing in an alarmingly devious manner. My adrenaline kicked in. I had to get up, I struggled hard. I had to get to my sister. I wasn't sure if there was anything I could do to help, but I was willing to die trying.

Finally on my feet, I stumbled forward as fast as I could. I fell twice before reaching them, each time earning applause and taunting encouragement.

"Come on dipshit, you can do it!" Their laughter fueled my rage. "We'll wait for you; we don't want you to miss any of the fun"!

I reached them just in time to see Randy push Joy's beautiful little face into the pile of shit that I managed to avoid moments earlier. He ground her nose deep into the vile mass, down to the earth beneath it. I could hear myself screaming, my voice had returned with a vengeance. He pushed himself back up to his feet, using her tiny body for leverage. Once up, he slapped the dirt from his knees. He turned to me and grabbed my face by the cheeks, squeezing hard, causing my lips to protrude.

"Any other tricks you'd like to try before we leave?" He asked, his face sporting a smirk and raised eyebrows.

I glared at him. He shoved my face back hard before letting go. Once again, I found myself on the ground. I did nothing. I just wanted them to leave.

"Come on Troy." He said as he gestured for him to follow . They ambled away down the path, laughing and congratulating each other on a job well done.

I scrambled as fast as I could to Joy on my knees. I rolled her over and grabbed her nose. I squeezed as I pulled down on it, in an effort to extract the poop. I quickly swiped my sleeve across her mouth. She parted her lips and gasped for breath. I used my thumbs to swipe the crap from her eyelids. She was coughing and frantically wiping at her face. I pulled her up into a seated position. She began to sob and gag. I frantically scoured through my pockets, in hopes of finding a Kleenex.

"What happened, are you guys OK!?!" A startled female voice asked from above us.

I looked up to find two teenage girls about Troy's age. They both gasped when they saw the condition of Joy's face. Both immediately started digging through their purses. One of them found a travel packet of tissues and dropped to her knees in front of us. She began frantically pulling them out of the little plastic wrapper. After wadding them together in her hand, she started wiping at Joy's face. The second girl unscrewed the bottle of water she was holding and offered it to the girl on her knees. She poured the water on the Kleenex and resumed her task.

"Oh my God! Who did this to you?!" She demanded in disbelief.

"Our brothers." Joy told her in a tiny and fragile voice.

"What?! Your brothers?!" She questioned in obvious disgust.

They offered to walk us home, but we declined. What if my parents were home? or worse yet what if they weren't?

We reluctantly headed for home. As we approached our house, we could see that neither of our parent's cars were in the driveway. That meant that the Beelzebub brothers were the only ones there.

I took Joy by the hand and led her around the back of the house. There was an egress stairwell that led to our finished basement.

I turned the knob and was relieved to find it unlocked. Pushing it open just a crack, I peeked in to see that it was dark. To the immediate left was our laundry room, it also had a full bath. I guided Joy through the darkness to its pocket door entrance. Once inside I slid it shut quietly and turned the knob to lock it. I flipped on the light and began removing our disgusting clothes, tossing them directly into the washing machine. I was really hoping that the assholes upstairs had the television on loud enough that they couldn't hear the shower turn on.

Once I was satisfied that the hot water and soap had sufficiently disinfected us, I turned off the water and stood silently, listening for any sign of movement. Nothing... I slid open the shower door and stepped out. I grabbed two large towels off the shelf and wrapped us each tightly in them. We sat down together on the fluffy blue bathmat, unsure of what to do next.

It ended up being one of the longest nights of our lives.

An hour had passed before it occurred to me that it was our parents' anniversary and that they wouldn't be home until tomorrow. Every year they would celebrate by spending the night at a luxury hotel. No wonder Troy and Randy took their torturous ways to a whole new level this afternoon.

At one point Joy got up suddenly and went over to the dryer. She pulled the door open as quietly as possible and looked inside. I told you she was a genius. It held a mixed load of underwear socks and pajamas. She immediately reached in and pulled out a yellow medium-length nightgown. Smiling from ear to ear, she turned to me and held it up.

"Look!" She whispered in a silent shout.

She found her panties and a pair of socks and put them all on quickly. I wasn't quite so lucky, so, I settled for one of my dad's T-shirts, it hung to my knees. We sat back down together on the blue bathmat and passed the time as best we could. We talked and giggled as quietly as possible and played "rock, paper, scissors" to the point of complete boredom. I don't recall ever playing it again after that evening. As the time passed our hunger became harder to ignore.

it was 2:00 AM, and I was sure the evil ones were asleep by then. I put my arm around Joy's shoulders and whispered to her.

"I'm gonna sneak up to the kitchen and get us something to eat!" I felt scared and yet somehow excited by the risk I was going to take. Her response left me feeling deflated and slightly stupid.

"No! Let's just get something from the storage room down here!" She whispered through a look of disbelief.

Again, I told you she was a genius. I couldn't believe I

hadn't thought of it myself, the basement pantry basically. I kissed her forehead and got to my feet.

"I'm going with you." She whispered as she jumped up.

She had a smile on her face as she practically skipped to the pocket door. Was she that bored? That she would risk another pummeling, as opposed to the safety of the laundry room? Apparently...

"OK, let's go! I felt ridiculously giddy as I quietly slid the door open just enough for us to exit. I took Joy by the hand and led her towards the storage room. We were tiptoeing and giggling.

"Where the fuck do you two think you're going"?

We jumped, screamed, and sprinted the rest of the way to the storage room. Randy jumped over the back of the couch to shorten the distance to his next attack. Troy was only a step behind. We turned and slammed the door shut as hard as we could. I held the knob tight, as Joy turned the lock just in the nick of time. They beat and kicked the door so hard, we thought it might come crashing in on us. Then it went quiet. We stood completely still and wide-eyed. Troy's voice broke the silence.

"Hope like it in there you two little retards! Cause you're gonna be in there until mom and dad find you!" He hollered through the door, paused a moment then added "And go ahead and tell them what happened! Because they're not gonna believe you! We'll have already told them the TRUTH! What little assholes you were acting like, and how we were trying to make you eat dinner and take a bath, but you refused and locked yourselves in the storage room. We tried everything to get you out! But you just wouldn't! It's amazing how stubborn you two can be!" They started laughing and I'm sure I heard a high 5 from beyond the door. "And don't bother thinking about opening this door, cause we're sleeping down here!... Or maybe we won't?... Not sure yet!" Again, they started laughing.

And so... we spent the rest of the night on a musty old sleeping bag, eating the household stash of Twinkies, raisins, and snack pack puddings.

It was about 10:00 AM before mom and dad knocked on the door, we opened it and were happy to be liberated... but we knew there would be consequences.

According to our older brothers, we still wouldn't come out this morning when told it was time to get ready for school. And of course, our folks believed them. They questioned us with heartbreaking disappointment... Why can't we behave when they're gone? Why did they always have to come home to some kind of trouble?

We were sent to our rooms and weren't to show our faces again until dinner. They punished us with a day free of Randy and Troy. Thanks mom and dad!

Obviously, our two big brothers, no, big bullies, made our lives miserable. They had a very complicated, yet brilliant way of manipulating and deceiving our parents. I still to this day, credit them with a certain twisted brand of genius. Not unlike the forms owned by the likes of Hitler, Jim Jones, or maybe Charles Manson. Our whole family was sucked into their cult, in one way or another. My folks didn't even know they were members. My sister and I knew all too well of our participation but saw no escape. We only had each other and a small hope for survival.

CHAPTER 22

RANDY

As a kid, Randy was a quintessential bully, and he looked the part. His hair was a sandy blonde buzz job, and he had one of those wide-shouldered stocky bodies, usually covered in a striped shirt that was at least two sizes too small. The permanent scowl on his face kept his grey eyes from ever looking fully open. I hated him then, and to date, have been given no incentive to change my mind. It's for these reasons that I'm still surprised I answered the phone one evening sometime back, knowing it was his number on the screen.

I was in the kitchen preparing a box of cheeseburger macaroni Hamburger Helper when the phone rang.

"Hello?" I answered in an obviously hesitant tone.

"Well hello stranger, it's been a while. Is this a good time?" She asked in a meek, barely audible voice.

I was instantly on the defensive. I wanted to scream into the phone... A good time for what?! To ask for money?! But I didn't.

"Sure, what's up with you guys?" I asked her, almost sounding like I cared.

"Oh, not much. Randy and I were talking the other night about how nice it would be if you paid us a visit. We haven't seen you in forever! Have you talked to your parents lately? Joy?"

She let out a nervous giggle before finally pausing to let me answer. I pretended and played along. I knew this wasn't just a courtesy call. They had a request, and I knew it involved my money. I lifted the lid of my nonstick frying pan to stir the cheesy noodles inside.

"Let me take a look at my calendar and see what's going on. I'll call you back and let you know if I have some time coming up soon. Maybe I can come down for a quick visit." I said with a condescending smile on my face, knowing full well that I had all the time in the world.

"Oh, that would be wonderful! Hope to hear from you soon. Bye for now!" She hung up a happy girl, her voice sounding confident and satisfied. She must have thought she pulled it off; she fooled me into thinking the call was for nothing more than to extend a friendly invitation. Lori never was the brightest bulb in the box. Hell, she married Randy, didn't she?

I knew I would be calling her back soon to tell her when I would arrive. Not because I wanted to see them, ever, but I had a morbid curiosity. I wanted to know what they wanted. And it would be my pleasure to disappoint them...

I was on my way to San Jose the following weekend. Percy dropped me off at the airport in the morning, and a few hours later, I was giving a cab driver Randy's address.

Lori opened the door before I could even knock.

"Hello, come in!" She invited, opening the door wide and gesturing me forward.

I stepped inside the simple but clean family room and put down my ratty suitcase. I was immediately uncomfortable.

"How was your flight?" She was wringing her hands nervously. "Would you like to sit down; can I get you anything?"

I almost felt sorry for her. She was an absolute wreck; it was pretty pathetic.

"Actually, I'd really like to wash up and use the bathroom," I said politely.

"Oh yes of course! Let me show you to the room you'll be staying in. It has an ensuite, so you'll have plenty of privacy." I followed her down a hallway. "There are clean towels and washcloths in a small linen closet to the left as you walk in."

"Thank you," I told her, smiling as I closed the door behind me.

I stood quietly for a moment surveying the room. I thought about pinching myself. I couldn't believe I was in Randy's house. I tried not to dwell on it, for fear of becoming physically ill.

I tossed my well-worn suitcase onto the bed, unzipped it, and retrieved my bathroom kit. I peed for what seemed like an unnaturally long time. It was great, better than the hot shower that followed. I put on the shorts, T-shirt and sandals I had packed in anticipation of the warm California weather. I decided to text Chuck before venturing out beyond the guest room.

ME: "Hey Chuck, just wanted to let you know I made it

here. I'll keep you posted on what's going on." I waited a few seconds.

CHUCK: "I can't wait to hear how it goes! Glad you had a safe trip! BTW, Boyd threw up all over the blanket that you keep on the back of the couch. The ugly knitted one your grandma made."

ME: "Just pick off the chunks and throw it in the washing machine. I'll text you when I know something." ...Waiting...

CHUCK: "OK, tootles for now!"

I stood up and put my phone in my pocket, then walked over to the door. I gripped the knob and found myself having to shake off a little nervousness before opening it. I took a deep breath and stepped into the hallway, exhaling as I walked towards the kitchen.

Lori was sitting at a small country-style dining table, sipping on what I assumed was a cup of coffee. When I entered the room, she looked up and smiled, then rose to her feet.

"Would you like something to drink? We have bottled water, soda, coffee, or tea. I'd be happy to make you a sandwich if you're hungry...."

"A bottled water would be great, thank you," I said as I walked around the table and took a seat.

Lori was a petite gal, about 5-3 at the most. She was slender and attractive. She had medium-length hair pulled back into a tight ponytail, possibly the only thing keeping her head from exploding. An oversized sweatshirt embroidered with a butterfly, and a pair of faded blue skinny jeans made up her wardrobe.

She grabbed a cold bottle of water out of the fridge and

handed it to me. She moved around the room nervously, looking for ways to keep her hands busy. I sat and watched her, thinking she might spontaneously combust or have a heart attack at any minute. She fired questions at me without waiting for a response. I had never seen anybody that highly-strung before. But I wasn't really worried about what she was doing or feeling. I wanted to know where Randy was.

Suddenly pulling out a chair, she sat down, joining me at the table. She offered me a cup of coffee. I didn't say anything, I just held the bottle of water up slightly. She gave a slight nod of embarrassment.

"Randy is going to be so happy to see you!" She exclaimed.

I decided to let her off the hook. I don't think she could have taken much more. After all, she had never done any-thing to me.

"Why don't we cut through the bullshit, Lori? What's going on, and why am I here? Why am I REALLY here?" I all but demanded.

It was incredible watching her face transform from prac-tically frantic to washed with relief. Her manner of speaking had also changed, from panicky to calm almost instantly.

"Your brother is very sick." (I could have told her that)

"What's wrong with him?" Again, sounding like I almost cared.

She explained that he was bedridden and in need of some extensive and expensive medical attention. There it was; the money was in the mix. Maybe I should have been ashamed that my first thought was of my money, not of what ailed my brother. Fact was, I didn't give a shit. I wanted to grab my thrift store suitcase and head for the airport. But it was too soon to do that. I still wanted to know what was wrong with the dumb bastard.

Lori pushed her chair back from the table and stood up.

"I'll take you in to see him." She waited for me to get up before turning towards the hallway.

I must have been pretty nervous myself; I could feel my heart start to race. I stepped around the table and followed her. She paused suddenly mid hallway and turned around to face me. Her voice was quiet and low. I had to lean in close to hear what she was saying.

"I just want you to know how hard it was for Randy to reach out to you. You'll be the first person to see him from your family in over four years."

I could feel my eyebrows raising. My curiosity was almost off the charts. Then she continued.

"I really need you to do me a favor. Please, try not to look or act shocked." She turned and continued down the hallway.

OK, now my curiosity was definitely off the charts. She stopped at the door and gave me a look I couldn't really read before turning the knob and pushing it open just a crack. Sticking her head in, she asked Randy if he was awake. I didn't hear him say anything, but she gestured me to follow her into the room.

"Look who's here honey!" Lori said enthusiastically.

I stood back from the foot of the bed. I kept my promise and didn't show any sign of shock. I think because I was in it. I just stood there and stared at him. I remember hearing Lori start what I'm sure she considered an ice-breaking conversation. I didn't catch a word of what she said. I was too busy gawking at him. I couldn't believe what I was seeing.

He covered the entire top of his Sealy Posturepedic king-sized mattress. I swear, he took corpulence to an entirely new level. There was a massive striped bedsheet strewn across his lap area. Thank God for that. His legs were touching each other yet were completely spread apart. Huge rolls of blubber were linked by deep crevices. I wondered how they cleaned down into their depths. Then again, maybe they didn't, judging by the smell of the room. His arms were resting at his sides, the fat making them stick out from his body. They closely resembled his legs. The crowning jewel of this human continent was his snowman-like head. His neck was gone, just a distant memory, not unlike his dignity. His eyes were slits like quarter moons, pushed nearly shut by his billowing cheeks. The oxygen tubes that ran from his nose squeezed his face, making little trenches. I couldn't help it. I was in complete awe. And I gotta say, I was loving it. Too bad Joy wasn't with me. She deserved this moment as much or more than I did.

"Good to see you Randy. You're looking well." I said through a supercilious smile. I could almost feel Lori wince.

"Yeah, good to see ya." He said flatly.

I stood and smiled, thinking that the old Randy would have beat me senseless for a smart-ass remark like that. But the new Randy was incapable of, well, anything! My smile widened.

"I think you two need to talk. I'll leave you alone for a while." Lori half suggested, half informed.

"Actually, that won't be necessary. I'll be leaving now." I announced with no further explanation.

I walked past Lori without making eye contact. I left the room and made my way down the hall to the guest room.

I put my toiletries back in the suitcase and zipped it shut. I called for an Uber and left the house to wait outside.

There was no way I was going to get involved in that episode of my 600-pound life. If they wanted to play bedridden victim husband and his enabling wife, they could call TLC.

CHAPTER 23

TROY

One evening not that long ago, the usual things were going on in our apartment. I was having a leisurely evening on the couch, and Boyd was having a leisurely evening lying on my stomach. Needless to say, we were both very annoyed when the phone rang. Come to think of it, anytime the phone rings. It's usually some telemarketer or somebody with a family matter. I preferred the telemarketers. Truth was, I didn't have a lot of friends, and I didn't give out my number freely, so if it wasn't Chuck... it had to be one of the other two.

"Hello?"

"Hi dear, it's mom."

"Hi mom. What's going on?"

"Well, I hate to tell you this, but auntie Rose died." She informed me, sadness in her voice.

"Oh, I'm sorry, mom. That's a bummer. She was a nice lady." I consoled her, even though I barely remember what auntie Rose looked like, having met her only maybe once when I was four.

"Thank you honey, she was my favorite aunt. The reason for my call is that we would like to see you at her memorial service this weekend, in Sacramento. Do you think you could make it down on such short notice?"

"Yeah, I'll check into it mom. I'll make some arrangements and call you back with my plans."

"OK baby, I'll be looking forward to your call. Love you."

"Love you too mom, talk to you soon"

Now, as you've probably guessed, I wasn't going to California to mourn auntie Rose. I was just so fucking bored with sitting around the apartment. I would have gone to a production of "little women" in Siberia.

The only problem now was I hated making travel arrangements. Searching for a flight, making a hotel reservation, blah blah blah. What do I do when I don't feel like performing a certain task? I find somebody else to do it for me. In this case, it would be a piece of cake passing the buck.

"Yes, how may I help you?" Chuck chimed into the phone with a giggle.

"Funny you should ask... I need you to make arrangements for a trip to Sacramento. If you do that for me, I'll take you with."

"For what date and how long!?" He squealed. I could hear a fast-paced thumping in the background.

"Chuck? Are you stamping your feet?"

"I can't help it! I'm really excited! Eeeee! I'm coming down there right now to make the arrangements!" Click.

Five minutes later my door opens and Chuck flounces in like it's Christmas morning.

* * *

Our Uber pulled up in front of the Trinity cathedral at 10:40. We stepped out onto the sidewalk into the warm morning Sacramento air.

"Oh my God, it's so beautiful and warm here!" Chuck announced joyfully as he raised his face and hands in the air and did a full spin.

"Take it easy Chuck. You don't wanna get sweaty before the service starts!" I teased him, and we both laughed.

We turned toward the church and started walking up the pathway to its entrance. That's when I saw him. He was standing to the left of a large hedge on the side of the building, smoking a cigarette.

"Oh shit!" I said under my breath while grabbing Chuck's arm. "See that asshole over there? That's my brother Troy... I don't wanna talk to him. Let's walk the other way." I turned to walk across the lawn, urging Chuck with a small tug to follow. But it seemed I was too late.

"I think he already saw you; he's headed our way," Chuck said quietly, trying not to move his lips.

"Fuck! let's keep walking!" I urged.

"Oh, stop it, just get it over with! You knew he might be here." Chuck said, trying to reason with me. I knew he was right.

I decided to stand my ground. I watched him as he walked towards us. He hadn't changed much, but I could see something different in his face. He didn't have the scowl anymore, and he was thinner. I felt my fear lessen as he got closer, and I could see his vulnerability. Not that I would show him any mercy... if what I saw was true.

"Hey kid, how you been? You look great!" Troy said with enthusiasm as he approached.

If I hadn't known better, I would have thought he was being genuine.

"Hello Troy. I'm fine, and you?" I said politely yet uninterested.

" It's kind of sad that people only seem to see one another at events like this one." He said in a sincere tone that I wasn't quite ready to believe.

"Hi, I'm Troy." He said while extending his hand towards Chuck.

"Chuck Barnes, nice to meet you!" I wasn't sure, but I thought I might have detected a little curtsy... I would laugh later.

"Well, we'd better take our seats. The service should be starting soon." I announced as I turned to walk up the steps of the church. I didn't want to run the risk of Troy trying to start a conversation.

I never asked about Troy or Randy over the years. I didn't give a rat's ass, and my parents knew it. As Joy and I got older, we got wiser. So did our parents. Gradually, as everyone's eyes opened wider, the truth about them became clear. It was quite strange actually. There were never any discussions about our fucked-up family dynamic. It just evolved slowly, until we all coexisted as a regular dysfunctional family. Eventually, us four kids all moved out on our own, and apart from Joy and I, didn't keep in touch. Every once in a while, a stray tidbit of information would escape from mom. Last I heard about Troy was that he was in a rehabilitation center, trying to kick some pathetic habit or another. I never bothered to ask for details.

The service was nice. Chuck bolted out the hymns with attention-grabbing enthusiasm. We gathered in the church commissary for a post-service luncheon, put on by the little old ladies of the congregation. About the time I couldn't stand it anymore, I spotted my mom.

"We're going to get going, mom." I said into her ear, then kissed her cheek.

"OK honey. Your dad and I would like you and Chuck to meet us for dinner tonight, would that be, OK?"

"Sure mom, call me with the plans."

I scanned the room in search of Chuck. I saw him across the room, socializing only as he can, thoroughly enjoying himself. Chuck is probably the only person I have ever met that can insert himself comfortably in any crowd... Whether it be a drag show in a dive bar full of gay drunks or a memorial service full of octogenarian mourners. I waved and caught his attention. He smiled and waved back; I could tell he was saying his goodbyes. He hugged all the little old people around him and headed towards me. They waved enthusiastically after him. He turned and blew them a kiss before we walked out the door. I called the Uber.

"Oh my God, that was so fun! I'm so glad you invited me!" He said as he leaned in for a shoulder squeeze to show his gratitude.

"You need help Chuck, but you're welcome." With that, I began my descent of the church stairs, Chuck in tow.

" Are you two ducking out early?" Troy's voice inquired from the right of the stairs. I felt the hair on the back of my neck stand up. We finished our descent and turned in his direction.

"Yeah, we're gonna get going, but you should go in and have something to eat. The ladies made some lovely salads!" Chuck suggested excitedly.

Once again, Chuck managed to make me smile at a very inopportune time.

"Thanks, I might do that," Troy said, looking a little puzzled. Turning his attention to me, he continued. "Say, I was hoping to have a quick word with you before you leave. Do you think that would be possible?"

"We're in a bit of a hurry, sorry." I blurted and started off toward the street to wait for the Uber. I stopped at the curb and looked back to see Chuck still talking to him.

"Chuck!" I was furious. He turned to me and held up his index finger, signaling for me to give him a minute. I don't think I had ever been more pissed in my life, than at that moment. The Uber pulled up beside me. Chuck continued to give Troy his undivided attention and didn't look over. I got in and told the driver to take me to the hotel. I glared in their direction as we pulled away.

I was sitting against the headboard watching an episode of Full House when Chuck walked in the room. I didn't say anything. I was afraid to. I hadn't cooled off enough yet. He walked over to the end of the bed and dropped down heavily.

"I'm sorry, I'm so sorry! But I just couldn't walk away from him. He seemed so sad!" I started to say something when he pleaded for me to listen first. "He explained to me what he wanted to talk to you about... do you wanna hear about it?"

"No! No, I don't wanna hear about it!" I practically screamed, instantly feeling kind of bad, because he looked so hurt. I calmed my tone and continued. "Look Chuck, I'm sure he gave you quite a sob story. And I know you're a very caring person, but you can also be a bit naïve. I've told you all the stories from when I was a kid. You know what he and my other brother did to me and my sister. I can't believe you even took the time to listen to his bullshit!"

"But I believe him. I really think he's changed!" He pleaded.

God help me, I couldn't believe what I was hearing. Chuck was siding with Troy. I'm sure he didn't see it that way, but that's how I felt. I had to be careful here. Angry words could lead to irreparable damage. Chuck was a special kind of people. When I told him he could be naïve, I fibbed a little. He WAS naïve, not could be. I decided it was probably best to humor him. I would listen. This is what he told me...in a nutshell...

Troy was down on his luck for the past 20 years. He had fallen in with the wrong crowd straight out of high school. It didn't take long before he found himself addicted to heroin and alcohol. He and his small gang of drug buddies lived communally in a small, rented apartment just outside of Los Angeles. They paid the rent with money they got from selling drugs and random robberies, mostly liquor stores. He spent a lot of his time in and out of jail. Then, one day about a year ago, he experienced his wake-up call. Yep, the life-changing wake-up call. That's where I interrupted Chuck's story.

"Stop... let me guess. He almost died blah blah blah and found God!" I spat the words.

Chuck looked at me with a dumbfounded expression, mouth gaping open.

"How did you know? Did somebody already tell you?"

"For God's sake Chuck, are you serious?"

"He just needs a little bit of money to get back on his feet! He even finished rehab!"

"He's full of shit, Chuck! He needs drug money!"

"No! I don't think so! You should have seen him. He was crying!"

"Look Chuck. I'm not changing my mind about this. I don't wanna hear one more word!" I demanded.

He got up and planted his hands firmly on his hips. "Fine!" Then stomped into the bathroom and slammed the door.

Troy died two months later. It was a combination of heroin and fentanyl. No, he didn't overdose. He was so fucked up, he walked in front of a bus.

JOY

As close as we were as kids, and as much as I love her, Joy and I just don't talk that much anymore. I would estimate two or three calls a year would be about it. We always exchange Christmas cards and phone calls on birthdays and vow to stay in better touch, but it never seems to happen. The last encounter we had in person was a visit I paid to her in Encino, shortly after our grandma died.

I took a limo from the airport to Joy's address. It was the last time I was in a limo. For some reason I decided to splurge. I still regret it, which is ridiculous. Sometimes I think about how much booze I could have bought with all that wasted money. Anyway, the driver pulled up to her house. He got out and walked around to the passenger side back door and opened it for me. I stepped out and waited for him to get my suitcase. I thought about how stupid it must have looked. Who pulls up in a fucking limo with luggage barely a step above a Walmart bag?

I was excited as I knocked on her door. It took me off guard when she opened it with her index finger pressed to her smiling lips, indicating we needed to be quiet. She waved me into the entryway and pointed to the couch across the room. A tall man with blonde hair was fast asleep, sprawled across the cushions. The sunlight from the front window washed over him, he looked quite cozy. Joy smiled lovingly as she looked at him. We stood silently for a moment before she led me into the kitchen, where we hugged and kept our voices low as we spoke.

"Did you have a good flight?" She whispered as she squeezed my hand. "Sit down. I'll get us a beer!" She returned to the table after grabbing two cold bottles from the refrigerator.

"Thanks," I said as I graciously accepted it. "Yes, the flight was good. My favorite part was exiting the plane." We both laughed quietly. She was aware of my dislike of air travel. I had always felt it was completely unnatural. Tons of steel should not be able to move through the sky.

"The handsome gentleman sleeping on the couch is my husband, Kyle. Normally he takes a nap in the bedroom after work. Today he made the mistake of sitting on the couch "just for a minute" you can see how that worked out." She rolled her eyes in mock irritation. "He owns and operates his own landscaping business, and it's taking its toll on him. He needs to hire more help." She said with a shrug and a smile.

The more we chatted, the more I was convinced she had never been happier. She and Kyle had plans to build their dream house just outside of town. They were talking about starting a family. I smiled at the thought of Joy being a mother. She would be an amazing mom. It was beyond exhilarating to see her so happy. Nobody deserved it more.

I planned on staying for most of the week. We had plenty of time to catch up, rehash, and get reacquainted. I told Joy I needed a little nap and a shower. She showed me to the guest room. It felt good to lay down.

We spent the next five days having a wonderful time. We saw the sights, ate in nice restaurants, and went for long walks. The night before my departure, we had a backyard barbecue and drank enough beer to drown a yak. We stayed up and laughed until dawn. I was having the time of my life. Kyle was a really nice guy and treated my sister the way she should have always been treated. He was affectionate and attentive, always thinking of her needs first. It seemed everything was perfect in my little sister's world.

I gave her a rib cracking hug before climbing into the cab. I rolled down the window and told her how much I loved her and that we should keep in better touch. We laughed because we knew we wouldn't.

"I have something for you." She said, handing me a sealed pink envelope. "Please don't open it until you're in the air, OK?"

"Sure, thank you." I smiled and blew her a kiss as the cab pulled away.

I watched her get smaller, and her enthusiastic wave finally disappeared as the cab drove further away.

My head was resting against the window as I stared down at the landscape of Idaho from 35,000 feet in the air. I still couldn't believe that it was possible. I tried not to think about it, but my mind kept wondering. What if the engines just suddenly turned off? Could we glide to a landing? Would we just fall out of the sky, straight down to our deaths? I looked up and was thankful to see the beverage cart getting closer. I reached down underneath the seat in front of me and pulled out my carry-on. I plopped it on my lap and started rummaging for my debit card, I wanted to be ready to pay for the cocktails I was gonna order. That's when I spotted the pink envelope. I had almost forgotten about it.

"Would you care for a beverage?" The stewardess asked, her hand already poised over the plastic beverage cups.

"Is there a limit on how many I can order at one time?" I asked.

From the expression on her face, I guessed that she had never been asked that before. She looked to the stewardess at the opposite end of the beverage cart, who answered with a shrug.

"I don't think there's a limit in first class." She said with a tone of uncertainty. "How many would you like?"

"I was thinking 4 bottles of Smirnoff and two cans of 7UP, and could you leave me a couple of those little cups full of ice?" I smiled at her with my best pleading look.

I started to hand her my credit card when she informed me that alcohol was complimentary in first class. I was pleasantly surprised. This was my first experience riding in the front section of the plane. Had I known that the seats were this much more comfortable and that everything was free, I might have done this before. I guess some things are worth the money.

I poured the entire contents of one of the little bottles over the ice and skipped the 7UP. I brought it to my lips and didn't put it down until the ice crashed into the bottom of my nose. I felt better already.

I opened the pink envelope. Instead of a greeting card, I pulled out a handwritten note. Expecting to see the words "I miss you already," followed by how great it was to see me again, how much fun she had and how we need to do it more often. Well, I was right about the first part.

CHAPTER 25

Joy's Letter

Oh my God, I miss you already!
but you knew I was going to say that!
LOL! I have some news to tell you,
I didn't want to say anything while
You were here, for fear of ruining our
good time. We found out very recently
that Kyle has liver cancer. He started
treatment last week. we have high
hopes. I will call you and fill you In
On the details in a couple days.
I haven't told mom and dad yet,
please don't say anything to them,
I hate for them to worry. I'll fill
them in when I know more.
love you! Xoxo

My heart sank. I had a lot of nerve thinking Joy's life had
finally turned around.

CHAPTER 26

BIG NEWS

I went to the DoubleTree hotel to meet my parents for breakfast. They were on a road trip heading for North Dakota, where they would attend a reunion of dad's old army buddies. They planned on staying in Missoula for a couple days and wanted me to show them around.

I walked in the restaurant and saw them seated at a table by the windows overlooking the river. Dad waved enthusiastically when he saw me.

"There you are, you're late! I thought we were gonna starve to death!" He laughed as he gave me one of his famous bearhugs.

"Hi mom!" I said as I leaned in for a hug and kiss.

We ordered breakfast and began discussing our itinerary for the day. Meanwhile, little did I know, Chuck had some plans of his own in the works.

***

Percy let himself free-fall backwards onto the puffy cushions of a large grey sectional.

"Oh yeah! this is the one!" He exclaimed with enthusiasm. Chuck rolled his eyes.

"Don't you think we should look around a little bit? I mean, that's the first one that you've sat on!"

Percy's aunt and uncle owned the Furniture Palace, a big warehouse in Lolo, about 10 miles out of Missoula. His uncle agreed to let him pick a sofa off the showroom floor and would deliver it and haul away the old one. The bill would be sent to me. It must be nice to have connections.

"OK, let's look around." Percy conceded but knew full well what their choice would end up being.

They toured the entire warehouse and sat on every single couch. After several arguments and bouts of pouting, they returned to the apartment and waited for the delivery guys.

I got home about 8:30 that evening. I opened the door and was met with the sight of an overweight gay man and a gargantuan Siamese cat sitting on a large, puffy, grey, L-shaped sectional.

"I see you did some shopping today," I said with a tiny bit of resentment in my voice.

"We did! What do you think?" He said cautiously.

"What did you do with the Big L?" I felt a little panicky. It was strange. I didn't realize before how attached I was to that stupid thing.

"They hauled it away, probably to the dump, I guess. Why?" His voice was full of curiosity, and I understood why.

I was acting like an immature little kid whose mom just threw away his beloved ratty old teddy bear.

"Just wondered."

With that I walked over and sat on its newness. It was quite comfortable and smelled nice. I decided I was going to hate it for a while. I've never been one for change, at least I think that's what my problem is. Maybe I just have unnatural emotional attachments to the couches in my life.

"I got some news today!" Chuck announced excitedly. He was smiling ear to ear and fidgeting as if he were ready to burst.

"Really, what?" He had my full attention.

"They found me a donor!" He squealed, jumping to his feet, and stomping them while spinning in a circle and clapping his hands.

***

David Wright was a 48-year-old married truck driver with three kids. He was making his usual drive between Evanston and Green River Wyoming one afternoon. He delivered parts between two auto body repair shops owned by the same man. There were days that he would make up to three round trips, filling up an entire workday, plus overtime. Up until that moment, all of his 12 years' worth of routine trips were quite uneventful, actually boring.

Liam Spector was a 29-year-old bartender from Cheyenne Wyoming. He was an unusually handsome man, which helped him make a good living off the tips he got from many smitten admirers at Carly's sports bar. He had spent his whole life being complimented and praised for his good looks. Thus, turning him into a raging narcissist. He drove alone that day on Interstate 80, listening to his favorite music, glancing at his phone, and checking himself out regularly in the rear-view mirror.

"Hello?" Liam answered his cell phone, after seeing it was Jillian, one of his many attractive admirers.

"I'm somewhere between Green River and Evanston. I'm not going to be back till sometime tonight." He informed her, sounding slightly disappointed. She must have extended an invitation that he couldn't possibly accept, due to his current distant location.

After a short and flirtatious conversation, he hung up and tossed the phone into the passenger seat. Just then, Pearl Jam began performing their song "Alive." Liam smiled and turned up the volume loud enough to drown out the sound of the Camaro's engine and the wind racing past his open window. It would be the last song he would ever hear.

David drove along I-80, listening to a local country radio station. He gripped the wheel with one hand and rested his deeply tanned forearm along the frame of the rolled down window. He stared directly ahead, watching the road disappear underneath the company vehicle. Tonight was pizza night with the family, and he was anxious to get home. Thinking about it brought a wide smile to his face.

The bee crashed into his cheek with a painful force and began flying frantically around the cab of the truck. David panicked and began desperately swatting at the drone, trying to direct it out the window. He thought about the EpiPen in the glove box in case he was stung. What he didn't think about, was the Camaro coming from the opposite direction.

* * *

"Give me some details, Chuck? What did the doctor say?" I asked him while using hand signals to direct him back down to the couch. He got the message and took a seat.

"There was a head-on collision somewhere in Wisconsin, and one man was killed instantly, and the other has been in a coma for over a month now." He performed the sign of the cross and continued. "The family of the man in a coma has decided to part him out."

"Jesus, Chuck!" I said with a wince.

"Sorry, but you know what I mean." He said apologetically, with an undertone of humor and a coy smile.

I shook my head.

CHAPTER 27

GRAMPS

I told Doctor Kelley that I had spent a lot of time the previous week rehashing childhood memories. I swear I saw her ears perk. I've always wondered why she was so interested in hearing about my family. It's probably because I never wanna talk about them and painstakingly avoid the subject. I guess that would pique anyone's curiosity. She asked if my reflections had been for a reason.

"Did something in particular happen to make you review your childhood? Is there anything I can help you resolve?" Her voice was hopeful. She wanted a story.

"No, nothing like that," I answered and watched her face fill with disappointment.

Maybe I just have too much time on my hands. But going over my past made me realize there were people I missed a lot. Mostly, my grandparents, I had considered my grandpa my best friend. I could talk to him about almost anything. Although I never brought up what was going on at home.

It's not that I didn't think he would believe me... I just didn't want him to worry, and I didn't want to make things even worse by snitching on Troy and Randy. So, I treated grandma and grandpa's house as a safe haven. I had always wished I could live with them.

* * *

If you hear the story from my mother, her parents were nothing short of Saints. They were hardworking, God-fearing people, quintessential pillars of their community. Grandma kept an immaculate house. It was filled with bathed, healthy children, folded laundry, and home-cooked meals. The beds were made daily, and bedtime stories read nightly. Weekends were spent family style. There were church picnics, family gatherings, and Sunday drives.

Grandpa worked as a family physician from 1948 to 1985, then retired at age 67. He acquired his wealth by investing wisely and saving diligently. This was a life of clean living and good fortune. Now, either my mom was a very lucky child, or she's confusing herself with Beaver Cleaver.

Now I can't remember what the circumstance was, but it required that me and Joy stay with Gram and Gramps for over a week. We were beyond happy to go. We considered it a well-deserved vacation from the pummelings.

One particular evening during our stay, Gramps and I found ourselves alone together. Gram wasn't feeling that great, so she went to bed quite early. Joy was spending the night with her friend Amy, a little girl she hung out with whenever we were there.

Grandpa recognized the situation as a good opportunity to break out his hugger-mugger bottle of Jack Daniels and turn on the History channel. As the night went on and Grandpa whittled away at his bottle, I was introduced to someone new. His name was "drunk Gramps", and he was as funny as hell. To this day, I'm not sure if all, or any, of his stories that night were true, but I knew I would never forget them.

He swirled his whiskey in a circular motion, then emptied the glass in one swift gulp. Actually, if memory serves, it wasn't a glass at all; It was an empty Cheez Whiz jar. Occasionally he would blow out a silent burp and refill whatever it was he was drinking out of. The crazy stories flowed right along with the whiskey.

According to Gramps, back in the 1950s, he was fiscally involved with the arrangement of a major marijuana production and distribution ring. He bragged about making thousands and thousands of dollars each harvesting season. He raised his processed cheese spread jar and toasted to never getting caught... especially by grandma. He explained that in the 50's, a first-time possession offense carried a minimum of 2 to 10 years in the clink and up to a $20,000 fine. (At the time, I wasn't altogether sure what he was talking about, but he had my full attention.) He pointed and winked at me.

"Reefer madness." He said matter of fact like, through an obvious slur. "1936 movie warning of the dangers of pot. You'll want to watch it. It's one of the most unintentionally hilarious movies ever made!" He said, slapping the side of his leg, laughing, and shaking his head. After actually seeing Reefer Madness several years later, I wondered if it was his way of warning me to stay away from drugs or if he knew I had a good sense of humor.

The 1960s saw a far less audacious grandpa. He ditched the weed scene; it was a bit too risky. He found a more convenient way to supplement his bankroll, and he could do it right from his practice, never having to leave the office. Writing prescriptions for recreational drug users and rich addicts wasn't quite as profitable as selling marijuana, but it was a bit less risky.

He refilled his little jar several times that night. I listened to his self-incriminating stories, and his admissions of moral inadequacy. I also laughed my ass off. It was so fun being with him, the both of us interacting as friends, not the way a grandchild and grandparent would normally. You would have thought my image of him would have been completely blown apart, that my respect and admiration would have all but disappeared. But it was on the contrary. I held him in the highest of regard. I was a bit too young to understand the magnitude of his recklessness and lack of ethics. All I knew was that he shared the unsharable with me, and only me.

Besides being quite the malefactor, Grandpa was a savvy businessman, or maybe just a really lucky one. In 1986 he bought 1000 shares of a new company stock called Microsoft, at $21 a share, and we all know the rest of that story.

His name was Ward Jenkins, but to me, he was Gramps. He died in 1998 and left me devastated. He left the rest of the family, or should I say vultures, waiting for grandma to join him. They were in for a big disappointment when it happened a year later. Guess who got the bulk of the estate?

CHAPTER 28

THE NIGHT BEFORE

Chuck decided he wanted to have a pre-operative party at Jaker's. It would just be me, him, and Percy. You don't wanna get too crazy the night before surgery, so he kept it small.

I stepped off the bus across the street from Jaker's and headed for the crosswalk. After successfully crossing, I walked up to the parking lot, at which point I could see Chuck and Percy waiting outside the door for me. Chuck began waving frantically as if he were afraid I wouldn't see him and just go home. I couldn't help laughing.

"There you are!" He said, clapping excitedly.

"Yep, here I am!" I teased him by mocking his excitement.

"Are you ready to have some fun?!" Percy asked as he held the door open for us. I followed Chuck in, and Percy pulled up the stern. The door floated slowly closed behind us.

"Will this work for you?" The waiter named Mike asked, as he gestured toward a booth by a window.

Chuck peered out the window and scanned the parking lot.

"Oh yes, this will be just fine! And Mike, thank you for picking a seat with a view. It's to die for! You're a doll!" Chuck gushed in sarcastic appreciation.

It caught me off guard, and I held my breath, waiting to see if his humor would be appreciated. Mike laughed and offered an alternative.

"There is a table for four in the bar, located conveniently close to the restroom, if you would prefer?" He suggested with a half shrug and a grin.

"That sounds fabulous, even better!" Chuck accepted gratefully with a giggle.

Mike seated us in the bar and handed us each a menu.

"Can I get you some drinks while you study the menu?"

"We have to study it? Will there be a test on it later?" Percy offered, apparently trying to join in on the smart-ass tone of the evening.

We obliged with a small round of courtesy laughs.

"I'd like a vodka 7 please." I said in a serious tone, hoping to break the cycle.

Percy ordered some big fruity drink with a straw and umbrella, while Chuck ordered a mudslide. It made me worry a little bit about the future of the evening.

In lieu of actual meals, we decided to order just about every appetizer on the menu. The booze flowed like wine, and the conversation never halted. Despite the upbeat mood, it was a bit of a task to hide my concern for Chuck. I didn't want him to sense my worry. It would freak him out. He's a bit superstitious and would probably take it as a bad sign. I did my best to act unconcerned. If Percy was doing that same thing, he was successful at it.

Chuck's doctor told him absolutely no food or drink after midnight. Our plan was to call it quits at 11:45. Both Percy and I questioned if taking a horrendous hangover with him to the operating table was such a good idea. He assured us he had it all worked out. He would be asleep by midnight, up at 6 am, and on the plane before 7:00. It's take off time. He would sleep it off during the flight... how far did he think Seattle was from Missoula? If you consider the time change, it was only a half an hour flight. He would be under the knife by 11:00 AM Pacific Standard Time. Knowing Chuck as well as I do, I questioned his plan. He made himself out to sound much more disciplined than he really was. I decided to keep my mouth shut, roll with the evening, and see how things went.

I'm not exactly sure, but I think it was somewhere in between our 6th and 8th drinks that Percy presented Chuck with a serious question.

"Chuck, honestly, are you scared?" He sat silently, trying to blink away his blurred vision, waiting for Chuck's answer.

Chuck's eyebrows raised and his lips pursed sideways, as he looked toward the ceiling. We guessed he was pondering his answer. Then he looked at us.

"No. If I could live through it being sawed off in a dark gravel alley in the middle of the night, with what could have possibly been a dirty butter knife... I think I can handle getting one sewn on by a bunch of sterile surgeons in a well-lit operating room."

He tossed his head back in a joyful laugh and lifted his glass in one hand, and faked jacking off with the other.

"To my longevity!"

His toast led to an evening of penis puns and jokes. We all raised our glasses in salute.

It was about drink#-9 o'clock when Aaron walked up to our table.

"Sounds like there's some fun being had over here, we could hear you from the other side of the bar!"

"Hi Aaron!" Chuck exclaimed, obviously glad to see his friend. "Who are you here with?" He added, craning his neck to see around the bar.

"Just a couple of friends here from Bozeman, nobody you would know," Aaron told him, dismissingly.

I may not be the most sensitive person in the world, but I could sense some tension. Especially from Percy. Aaron stood next to the table smiling for a few moments before excusing himself.

"Well, just thought I'd stop by and say Hi on my way to the bathroom. You all have a nice evening." With that, he walked away, but not before winking at Chuck. The tension I sensed from Percy was verified when he stuck his tongue out and flipped him off as he walked away.

"I hate that asshole!" Percy hissed.

"You hate everybody Percy! You're just jealous because he shows me attention. That's no reason to hate somebody!" Chuck countered, sounding more than a little smug.

"Aaron's a greedy pig! He's a fag when it's convenient, the rest of the time he chases pussy... or anything willing!" He spat the words in disgust.

"Bullshit Percy, don't make up lies about people!"

This was getting out of hand; we were supposed to be having a good time. I decided to intervene.

"Knock it off you assholes! Not tonight!" I demanded. "One more word about Aaron and I'm gonna leave, I mean it!"

It was just about that time that Aaron was making his return trip from the bathroom back to his table. He smiled and walked by without stopping. Chuck and Percy were locked in a temporary "glare down". If looks could kill, it would have all ended in a murder-suicide, Percy would be declared the perpetrator. I gave them both another look of warning. We ordered another round, and a plate of Jaker's famous onion rings.

I thought things had cooled down pretty good and everybody was getting along. I know I was having a really good time, but apparently, there was still some resentment bubbling under Percy's collar.

"Hey Chuck, do you think if we asked Aaron what the LGBTQ is, he could give a STRAIGHT answer?" He said smiling before shoving another whole onion ring into his mouth.

"He's not bi Percy!" Chuck said angrily, wiping tartar sauce from the side of his mouth.

"I know Chuck, that's my point! He's a big fat straight pervert! He'd fuck anybody, or anything for that matter!"

That was it for me. I wadded up my napkin and threw it in the middle of the table.

"I'm out of here, I don't need this shit tonight."

I settled the bill with Mike, and gave him a generous tip, he earned it. I told Percy and Chuck that I would be waiting outside for my Uber. They were welcome to join me if they could keep their fucking mouths shut, long enough to make it home.

I stepped out into the night air, what a relief, I hadn't realized how stuffy it was in the bar. I took a deep breath; it amplified my buzz. I lit a cigarette and leaned against the building, watching for my ride. I let out a billowing plume of smoke just as Percy walked out the glass door, causing him to wave his hand in front of his face while trying to dodge it. I apologized.

"Are you joining me?"

He nodded his head and stood silently with his arms folded. Not but a second later, Chuck joined us. The Uber pulled up and we all got in. The trip home was eerily quiet. Thank God.

I set my alarm for 5:30 the next morning. I wanted to make sure Chuck got up on time. I went upstairs to his apartment and knocked on the door. Surprisingly, he answered it.

"Good morning, come in!" He chimed. He was showered and shaved, ready for the day.

"Wow, I'm impressed. I was expecting to have to drag you out of bed!" I told him as I walked through the door. "I don't think we should wait, as long as you're ready I'll call an Uber now."

We stood outside the apartment building and waited for his ride. He was fidgety with excitement. I was glad to see he wasn't scared.

"Would you water my African Violet in a couple days?" He suddenly blurted wide-eyed, it must have just popped into his head.

"OK, but you might want to text me a reminder."

His expression turned to relief. I couldn't believe he was worried about a plant, and not having surgery in a couple hours. That's Chuck for ya.

The Uber pulled up and stopped right in front of us. I grabbed for the door and pulled it open. Chuck tossed his small duffel bag onto the seat and slid in beside it.

"This is it, wish me luck!" He said, then blew me a kiss.

"Good luck Chuck. Have a safe flight and let me know when you get to the hospital."

I closed the door behind him. He waved at me as the car pulled away, I stood and watched until it was out of sight.

CHAPTER 29

WHAT IF?

"Doctor Kelley is ready for you now," Teresa informed me.

I looked up at her to make sure she was talking to me. She nodded. I was reading "life in these United States" in the Reader's Digest. I dog eared the page. I'm not sure why. Maybe I was planning on stealing it on my way out?

When I stepped in the office, Doctor Kelley was busy writing in a small notebook. I didn't say anything as I walked past her desk and took my seat on her new crappy love seat. After a moment or two, she laid down her pen and looked up at me.

"So, how have you been since last week?" She asked while folding her hands in front of her.

"Well, not too bad. Chuck is in the hospital in Seattle. He finally had his transplant surgery."

Her eyebrows raised in curiosity.

"Is that right, how did it go? She asked with genuine interest.

"The procedure went well, but anything can happen. We'll just have to wait and see; I definitely have my fingers crossed."

She must have sensed the excessive concern in my voice.

"Your worry is understandable. But somehow, I sense there's more to this story. Am I wrong? She questioned.

I swear this woman was really in her niche. It was as if she could read me like a book. Truly unbelievable.

I told her I had spent some time since our last visit contemplating life and mortality. I told her I had recently begun worrying about what was around every corner.

"Are you concerned about dying?" She asked.

"Well, I can't say I'm looking forward to it, but that's not what I'm getting at," I assured her.

She asked for an example. I told her that every moment seemed like an example. She gave me one of those what the hell are you talking about looks, and her brow furrowed to the middle of her crinkled-up nose. I told her that I saw some stupid kid fall off his bike the other day. A lady was walking her dog on some grass across the road, and he got off his leash. Spot ran across the street and jumped up onto the sidewalk directly in front of the bike. The kid hit his brakes, wavered, and took a nasty spill. Doctor Kelley shook her head slightly to show she still wasn't following. I continued.

"If that stupid kid had just took out the trash, like he was supposed to, he would have been 5 minutes later, and never even would have seen that dumb dog." I explained. She decided to elaborate on my thought.

"Or maybe if that woman had taken her dog to the park instead of finding a place for him to crap on the side of the road, the dog wouldn't have seen the kid and took off after him." She ended her statement with a shrug.

"Hey, whose example is this anyway?" I said in a terrible Italian accent, while waving pinched fingers in her direction.

She laughed and apologized jokingly.

"Look, you can't do that. It's just life, a series of actions and reactions. There's no avoiding them. "What if's" don't exist." She said still smiling.

And just like that, I'm cured. I thought to myself, performing an internal eye roll.

I decided to share a real story with her. It was an experience from my childhood that still haunts me to this day. I hate talking about it but telling it to her seemed the only way to make her understand the magnitude of my disdain for the unknown. It seems the runaway dog and the stupid little shit on the bike story didn't cut it. Maybe Astoria would help her understand.

CHAPTER 30

ASTORIA

The Carlsons were next-door neighbors of ours for several years while growing up. Me and Joy were regulars at their house on weekends. It wasn't that we liked them all that much, or that they were much fun, but it was better than being at home. Shawn and William were twins. If memory serves, I think they were a year ahead of me in school. They weren't too thrilled about Joy always tagging along with me. They thought she was too young. They tolerated her so that I would stay. Like I mentioned, they weren't all that much fun to be around, so they probably didn't have a lot of alternative friends.

One afternoon during the summer of my 5th-grade year, William Carlson showed up at our front door. He was absolutely giddy as he told my parents that I was invited on a trip to Astoria, Oregon, with him and his family. This was the first that I had heard of it. They accepted the invitation for me even before consulting with William's parents, or with me for that matter. It was lucky for me that I actually wanted to go. There was no mention of Joy. I was a little concerned about leaving her home alone, but I went. I had hoped my mom and dad would keep a better eye on her in my absence.

We arrived in Astoria late in the afternoon on a Friday. Because it was like a million years ago, I may be a little sketchy on some of the details. I do know that Mr. Carlson had reserved two rooms in a small motel, one for him and Mrs. Carlson, and one for us kids. I remember how excited we were. There was a TV in the room and a number of vending machines just outside the door. We planned on eating a bag of everything from A-Z, and a can of each kind of soda. It was so cool to have a room of our own. I remember feeling kind of grown-up.

When we woke the next morning, Astoria was completely fogged in. I had never seen such thick fog before in my life. It was like everything around that little motel had fallen off the face of the earth. The Carlsons took me out to breakfast, over which they discussed postponing our walk to the beach. Such talk didn't go over well with Shawn and William. They argued, whined, and stomped stubborn feet in objection. I just sat there and ate up the bacon. Man, that was good bacon. That I remember vividly. In the end, they caved and decided we were going to head for the beach; Maybe the fog would lift a bit by the time we were done eating. I guess pitching a hissy fit worked in this family.

I recall my pant legs getting wet as we walked through the thick grass of the dunes. The dense fog surrounding me filled me with mixed emotions, scared shitless and totally excited at the same time. I think everybody else was feeling something similar, you could almost smell the adrenaline in the air... Except for Mrs. Carlson, that is, I think she was only getting the scared shitless part.

It wasn't long before we heard the roar of the ocean growling louder. The fog hadn't budged. Even back then, I was pretty sure that the whole situation was a bit iffy. As soon as we hit the flat sand, Shawn and William took off towards the sound of the surf. My hesitation suddenly vanished. I remember an adrenaline rush of my own, and the next thing I knew, I too, was off and running. I could hear my own laughter and feel my heart pounding as I desperately tried to keep up with my own legs. It was pure exhilaration. I never had felt it before and haven't since.

We had to halt abruptly at the edge of the waves. They were barely visible through the fog. They made a soft lapping sound as they rolled in one after another. It was a tranquil moment that was quickly shattered. The elder Carlsons were quickly upon us, scolding as they approached. We were to all stay together. The poor visibility and the unpredictability of the ocean required our utmost caution. It was only a matter of minutes before the three of us were skipping along the waterline, well ahead of the folks once again. We bounded along laughing, and stopping occasionally for a seashell or two. I felt truly happy. That didn't happen to me all that often.

William had gotten quite a bit ahead of Shawn and me; we had been distracted by a slimy heap of sea kelp, out of which we each chose a "bulb whip" to twirl over our heads. We could barely see his silhouette through the fog. As we moved closer, leaping and twirling the kelp vines like lassoes as we ran, he became clearer, and we could see that he had stopped and was looking down at something near the water's edge. I sprinted up behind him, panting like a dog, smile still plastered from ear to ear. It faded quickly. My prized clamshell and kelp whip fell back to the sand. Shawn soon raced up behind us, using his outstretched arms against our backs to help him come to a stop. It made William and I lurch forward in horror. Shawn was still laughing as he looked down, but quickly froze when he spotted the gruesome sight.

Our eyes were assaulted by what I would describe now as a white, bloated, and tattered flesh, clinging too broken and denuded bones. There was shredded fabric around what may have been the torso area, yet there was no torso. There was still part of a skull, it had no face or flesh left but there were sporadic locks of long dark hair clinging onto it, here and there. Small crabs were climbing in and out of the crevices. I remember hating them, thinking that they shouldn't be doing that. Mr. and Mrs. Carlson reached us just as William fainted. I'll never forget the sound of Mrs. Carlson's blood-curdling scream.

The next thing I knew, I was being pulled away from the horrific scene. I could feel a hand clamp around my arm and being pulled. My eyes were locked on the poor remains, my mind was reeling in disbelief, and I couldn't look away. Then suddenly, I was spun in the other direction and was led off the beach, through the creepy dunes, and back to the quaint little hotel room with the TV and vending machines. Somehow, the room seemed different as we sat on the bed and listened to Mr. Carlson talk to the police. It had lost its charm. Any guilt I felt about leaving Joy at home disappeared. I was really glad she had missed this experience. We headed home that day, cutting our trip short by two days. Nobody really saw the point in trying to have fun after that. The long drive home was somber and quiet.

* * *

Jim Martin was a recently retired dentist from Boise, Idaho. He and his wife Shelly had booked their Holland America line Pacific Coast cruise a year in advance.

It had been a long wait, but they were finally aboard the ship. To say they were excited would be a gross understatement. The room was beautiful, but they weren't in it very long. Just long enough to settle in and unpack their suitcases for the week. They intended on utilizing every amenity and participating in every activity available. And that's what they did... for the first three days anyway.

Jim woke up later than usual on the 4th morning of their adventure. He rolled over to see if his wife was still sleeping. Her side of the bed was empty. Figuring she must be in the bathroom, he closed his eyes and waited for his turn. He drifted off and didn't wake up again for another two hours. He got up and went to the bathroom to see if she was in there, it was empty. He was starting to feel a little alarmed but tried to rationalize. Maybe she had gotten up super early and went down to read the newspaper and order a coffee. No need for concern.

By noon he was in full-blown panic. He felt like he had searched the entire ship before having her paged. She didn't respond to it...

Shelly woke up early to a beautiful sunny morning. Jim

was still sound asleep, and she would let him stay that way. He deserved the rest. She decided to grab her book and go down to the pool, stretch out on a lounger, and read. She grabbed her camera and hung it around her neck before leaving the room; she wasn't gonna let this vacation go undocumented.

None of the amenities were open at the pool yet that morning, but there was a fresh supply of oversized towels stacked on a counter at the bottom of the stairs. Shelly grabbed two of them, selected a lounge chair, and spread one of them across its surface. Nobody else was up that early, so she found herself alone on a luxury cruise ship sitting by a sparkling pool. Heaven on earth.

After a couple chapters of Stephen King's latest novel, Shelly got up to stretch. She walked over to the side of the ship and noticed a pod of killer whales. Understandably excited, she hurried back to the lounger and grabbed her camera. She clicked away, delighted that they seemed to be cooperating, almost posing. That's when she decided to step up a couple of rungs on the railing. A little higher up would enable her to get even better shots. Nobody saw her go over the edge. Nobody heard her screams from the water below. The ship forged ahead, leaving Shelly Martin in the Pacific Ocean to drown. Three days later, they called off the search.

That was the story they pieced together from the evidence Shelly left behind. Her bed had been slept in, so they knew she must have gotten up early. The empty lounger covered with a towel and a bookmarked novel. Her camera was not in the room. It wasn't down at the pool. It must have gone over the side with her. Mr. Carlson had come to our house to fill us in on this information, thinking maybe it would give me some closure. It definitely answered a lot of my questions, but it also introduced me to the world of "What if's." They would haunt me my entire life.

What if Shelly didn't wake up early that morning? What if she had forgotten her camera in the room? What if the whales had swum in a different direction that day? What if it had been raining? What if, what if, what if...

Would Shelly still be alive today? Or was it her time, and if she hadn't done any of the things she did that morning, would God have found her anyway?

THERE'S NO PLACE LIKE THE HOME

I had made a drunken promise to Chuck the night of his pre-surgery party. I told him that I would fill in for him at blushing meadows during the four Sundays he would be in Seattle. I've really got to quit drinking and talking. Chuck knows that I would rather snort piss than step foot back in that place. He took me up on it anyway. It proved how much he cared about his patients and his volunteer duties. Oh, what the hell, it's only four visits. I told myself to buck up and just do it.

Not much had changed since the last time I was there. I must admit I was a bit uncomfortable and felt a bit sheepish when I first passed through the grimy glass double doors. Mean old Marianne was still staffing the reception desk. She looked up at me, a look of smugness washed over her face.

"Couldn't stay away huh?" She practically laughed, through her thin-lipped smile.

"Trust me when I say I have no problem staying away from here, especially the reception desk." I hissed back at her.

I headed for the cafeteria to assist with breakfast service. Nothing had changed. The old folks bitched about the food, and occasionally spit some of it up. Actually, something was different... I didn't have Chuck to exchange frustrated and disgusted looks with. Once I got a reasonable amount of food down most of the geriatric diners, it was clean up time. I didn't mind cleanup time, I could handle filling up bus tubs and wiping tables, at least I was alone.

After finishing up in the cafeteria, I reluctantly went to Marianne's desk to be assigned my next task. I could see the evil grin on her face as I approached.

"Are you ready for some real fun?" She said in her most practiced condescending voice.

"Sure, lay it on me Marianne!" I answered with faux excitement.

"All of the public access bathrooms on this floor need a deep cleaning... that's where you come in!" She informed with a broad smile and a wink.

I'm sure she thought she was really sticking it to me, that I would be horrified. But the joke was on her, I didn't mind any task that required solitary confinement. I certainly didn't tell her that, for fear she would change her mind and do something really wicked, like have me help the activities director.

I was about an hour away from freedom. I had my toilet wand feverishly scrubbing under rims and swishing Comet clouded water. I had two more restrooms to go and would make sure they each took 30 minutes to clean. I had it all figured out. As I headed toward my next conquest, some stupid young girl in scrubs holding a clipboard rained on my parade.

"Hi there, Marion told me that you are to quit with the bathrooms and go to room 217 for a resident visit." She informed, as if delivering good news. Roy Butterfield had joined the blushing meadows family three weeks earlier and hadn't received a single visitor.

I walked to the janitorial closet as slowly as I could, feeling not only defeated, but really pissed. I practically threw the cleaning tote inside the door, then slammed it shut. I muttered profanities all the way down the hall on my way to 217.

I stood outside the door that separated Roy Butterfield and myself. I watched him through the pane of glass at the top of it. He was seated at a small square table pushed up against a rain-drenched window. From the position of the cards he was manipulating, I assumed he was playing solitaire. I knocked lightly on the glass porthole. He turned his attention towards the faint pounding. His eyeglasses rode low on the tip of his nose as his eyes peered over their rim. His hair was white and parted cleanly to one side. He wore blue jeans, a green sweatshirt, and a new pair of expensive sneakers. With a wave of his hand, he gestured for me to enter. He had a wide sincere smile, which made deep lines form at the edges of his eyes. I was relieved to see that he at least appeared friendly. I also noticed he seemed a bit younger than most of the other residents.

I made my slightly reluctant way in and closed the door behind me. Roy greeted me with a hearty hello and pointed to the chair across from his. I shook his hand and took a seat.

"The receptionist told me this morning that I would be

getting a visitor. I've been looking forward to meeting you all day." He said sincerely.

"Well, it's nice to be here, thank you." I smiled back.

He seemed lonely. I could sense it in his body language and his tone of voice. What I hadn't sensed, was his seemingly tortured soul.

Roy told me that he and his wife Ella had raised their family here in Missoula. He spent his career as a barber, and Ella was a high school math teacher. They had a comfortable home on the outskirts of town and spent most weekends on camping trips with their kids. To that point, it sounded picture-perfect, almost boring.

Eventually the kids grew up, and one by one moved out of state. They both retired and spent a few years traveling, until Ella was diagnosed with pancreatic cancer. She died the following year. Roy was understandably devastated by her loss. He sold the house and moved into an apartment not far from his eldest son Craig in Cedar Park, Texas, outside of Austin.

His mood shifted again. It seemed to darken. Even his body language changed. It was as if he had shrunk a size. He leaned in close as he spoke to me. He continued his tale with how he would spend every Sunday at Craig's house. Craig was married to a lovely woman named Shannon. They had three school-aged children, Danny was the oldest, then Julie, and the youngest was a small boy named Jamie. Roy looked over at the closed door, as if to assure our privacy, then straight into my eyes.

He began by telling me everything was wonderful in the beginning. The visits were the highlight of his week, always looking forward to the fun they had together. They would all enjoy an early dinner and play a board game or watch a movie afterward. Suddenly, he paused and swallowed hard enough to be audible. Apparently, during one particular visit, things changed. Roy told me he could tell something was wrong. The whole mood in his son's household was odd, tense, and had a sense of iniquity. I felt my head cocked to the side, and my eyebrows skyrocket as I questioned his meaning. His face seemed to turn to stone, and he leaned in even closer. He told me in a very flat tone that he believed his grandson, Danny had become possessed by a demon, if not the devil himself. I'm sure my expression intensified.

My 60 minutes of in-room visitation was close to up for the day. I decided to stay anyway. He had me quite intrigued. I didn't want to wait another week to hear the rest of his story.

"Grandpa, do you want to see my new room?" Danny asked Roy enthusiastically.

"Well of course I do!" He said as he stood up to follow his grandson up the stairs.

Danny opened his bedroom door and told his grandpa to come on in. Roy said the minute he stepped in the room, the strange feeling he had been experiencing since he got there intensified tenfold. He said the boy walked over to a small writing desk and took a screen lid off a small fish tank. There was a tiny white mouse running on a wire wheel. Danny reached in and pulled the rodent out by his tail and dangled it in front of his face.

Roy paused for a moment and rubbed his open palm across his forehead. He clenched his fists and placed them in front of himself on the table. He continued talking; his voice filled with disbelief.

"He bit the poor little thing in half! He lowered it to his mouth, and then with one quick snap of his jaw, he was chewing on it! I'll never forget the maniacal look on his face!" Roy gasped the words, trying hard not to break into tears. "After he swallowed it, he did a little kind of jig, smiling and staring straight into my eyes." Roy lifted his fists and brought them down hard on the desktop. "Then he popped the other half in his mouth as if it were the last bite of a juicy hamburger." He couldn't hold it any longer and began to sob.

I could feel horror and disgust paralyzing my face. I managed to ask him through my nausea in a strained voice,

"What did you do?!"

He lowered his head and stared at white-knuckled fists. He was silent for several moments. I thought he looked like he might be praying. Finally raising his eyes back to mine, he spoke.

"I ran back down the stairs. I was hysterical. I must have looked like a madman. Even after viewing all the damning evidence, including an empty mouse cage and blood spots on Danny shirt, they didn't believe me." He covered his face and sobbed even harder.

Over the course of the next year, Danny pulled off several fiendish acts that Roy was a witness to and probably several he didn't. He said he repeatedly tried to convince Craig and Shannon that there was a grave problem with the boy. Nobody would listen to him. It seemed as if the situation was purposely being ignored. Roy could only guess that Danny's parents saw him as mentally ill, not possessed. They were trying to spare him from spending his life in a mental institution. Roy told me that he knew the difference; he knew deep down in his heart. The boy was possessed, not insane.

I wasn't sure if I believed Roy Butterfield's story, but I was pretty fucking sure that he did.

VISITING HOURS

Percy had flown out to Seattle to spend a week with Chuck after his operation. The plan was that I would go out and spend some time there after he got back. Somebody had to be here to take care of Boyd.

I arrived in Seattle at 10:00 AM and took a cab straight to the hospital. I stopped off at the gift shop and bought some flowers and some sort of stuffed animal. I wasn't sure if it was a cat or a bear, but I knew he would like either one. The nurse on his floor directed me to his room.

Flowers in one hand and mystery stuffed animal in the other, I stood for a moment and observed him through the glass at the top of the door. He was watching "The Young and the restless", his favorite soap. He looked pretty content, I almost felt bad about interrupting him. I pushed my way through the door and held the gift shop purchases in his direction.

"Sorry to interrupt!" I announced through a huge smile. It was good to see him.

"Oh my God!" He squealed, stretching his arms out to receive his gifts. "I can't believe you're here!"

"That's strange, since I told you I was coming Chuck," I said in jest.

"I know but I'm just so excited! He squeezed the toy and took a deep sniff of the mixed flowers. "Thank you so much!"

After admiring them for a few seconds, he invited me to take a seat in the chair beside his bed.

"Have you got a room yet? Cause if you want to, Ma said you could stay at her house." He said, through the flowers still wedged under his nose.

"That was nice of her, but I have a room over at the Travelodge, it's really close. I'll be sure to thank her for the invitation when I see her." I told him, secretly relieved to decline.

I spent the bulk of the next three days with Chuck in his room. We watched television, worked crossword puzzles, and occasionally took wheelchair walks around the hospital. Once a day I would go out and bring back takeout food. My visit flew by, and it was time to head back to Missoula.

I checked out of my room and had the Uber driver go through Jack in the box before heading to the hospital. My flight didn't take off until 4:00 PM that afternoon, so I could spend most of the day with Chuck before leaving.

"Good morning!" He said enthusiastically, directed more at the bulging bag of fast food in my hand, than at me.

I took my seat beside his bed and handed him his breakfast. He began pulling out various wrapped sandwiches, sauces, and napkins.

"Didn't you get any hash browns?" He asked in amazement.

"Are there any in the bag?"

"No!" He blurted in disbelief.

"I'm not sure, but if there aren't any in the bag..."

" Shit!" He cut me off. "They're my favorite part of the breakfast menu!"

I rolled my eyes at him, and he tried to throw a napkin at me, it fluttered to the floor. It made us both to laugh. He could be such a dumb ass.

As we unwrapped our selections, the door swung open, and Chuck's mom walked in.

"Well good morning you two, hope I'm not interrupting!" She announced as she entered, carrying a McDonald's bag in one hand and a magazine in the other.

"Looks like I'm a little too late, you already have breakfast." She looked a little disappointed.

"Look in the bag Ma, are there any hash browns?!" His face filled with hope.

"I think so, honey." She said handing him the bag.

He dug through it, almost frantically, in search of the greasy deep-fried potato treat.

"Yes!" He exclaimed as he pulled one from the bag.

"I finished this issue of better homes and gardens, and I thought you might like to look at it." She said as she held it out to him. He looked a little puzzled as he reached for it.

"I don't read Better Homes and Gardens Ma," He told her, his voice flooded with sarcasm.

"Let him know when you're done reading the current issue of Teen Beat, Mrs. Burns," I said through a laugh. She didn't seem to get the joke, but Chuck did, and snarled his nose at me.

I was starting to question my decision to get an afternoon flight. I wasn't sure how we were gonna fill up the rest of the day without my eyeballs rolling out of my head. Mrs. Burns decided she would stay until I had to leave, so she could drive me to the airport. I would just have to buck up and try not to kill either of them.

It seemed to take longer than usual, but three o'clock finally rolled around. It was time for me to leave.

"Looks like we better get going," I said to Mrs. Burns. She smiled and nodded in agreement.

"Can't you just stay another day?!" Chuck whined.

"I can't, I'm covering for you at the home tomorrow." I reminded him.

"Oh yeah." He said through a frown and tears welled in his eyes.

"Oh, for God's sake Chuck! You're gonna be home in two weeks! Knock it off!"

"I'm sorry, I know, but I'm still sad!" He said, before a letting out a full-blown sob.

I pulled open the door for "Ma", and she stepped into the hallway. Before I could follow, Chuck called after me. I turned and looked back at him. He was holding up the stuffed animal I had brought him.

"Is this a bear or a cat?"

CHAPTER 33

NEVER DRINK ALONE (in public)

I walked down the steep cement stairs to my apartment, unlocked the door, and went inside. Percy was on one end of the couch watching TV with his head laid back against a pillow that he had propped up against the wall. Boyd was stretched out on his side, and pretty much took up the rest of the sectional. Percy lifted his hand in a half-assed wave and Boyd only opened one eye in acknowledgment of my homecoming.

I took my suitcase to the laundry closet and emptied it into the washing machine, put my bathroom stuff away, and shoved the suitcase back into its place underneath my bed. I went out into the living room and sat on the chair across from the two balls of fire on the couch.

"So, anything exciting happened while I was gone?" I said, checking to see if they were alive.

"No, not really," Percy answered, I could tell he had to muster up the energy just to answer me.

"What the Hell's the matter with you two?" I asked, sounding a bit annoyed.

Percy's head rolled slowly in my direction, and he looked at me for a few seconds before answering, as if he were processing my question.

"We're just tired. We stayed up late watching movies." His head rolled back toward the tv.

Being as the company was quite lacking that evening, and that Chuck was doing so well, I decided to go out and have a few celebratory drinks.

I wasn't sitting at Sean Kelly's bar for much more than 10 minutes before the intrusion. Chris Ryan and his longtime girlfriend, Connie, bellied up to the bar beside me. I probably wouldn't even have noticed, except for the attention-getting elbow Chris fired into my side. They invited me to join them at a table, and I reluctantly did so. I'm so stupid.

"So, what have you been up to, I don't think we've seen you for a year or two!" Chris commented as he pulled out a chair for Connie.

"Yeah, that sounds about right." I retorted with fake enthusiasm and took my place at the table.

Chris took his seat and signaled for the waitress.

"What can I get for everybody tonight?" The waitress called Becky asked as she poised her order pad.

"How about a couple pitchers of bud light and three chilled glasses?" Chris said, smiling up at her.

"Sounds good. I'll be back in a minute." She answered.

It was true that I hadn't seen the two of them for a few

years. Frankly, I hadn't given either one a fleeting thought in as long. I guess you could say they fell into my acquaintance category. I decided before taking my seat that I was going to try and be pleasant and open-minded, not my usual self. I would at least pretend to be enjoying our unexpected, un-invited, and unwelcome reunion. It didn't take long for them to challenge my good intentions.

I was in the middle of a long swig of the cold beer when Connie blurted out her eloquently put opening statement.

"We heard you inherited a lot of money. Is that true?"

I took my time drinking and swallowing the beer. It would give me a few seconds to decide on my retort. I hadn't seen her in a while, so I couldn't remember if she was a rude bitch or a dumb bitch.

"Well, Connie, it's true that I was blessed to have inher-ited a part of my grandparents' estate. Why do you ask?" I answered somewhat cautiously.

Their questions came at me as if fired out of a nail gun. The sting was there, but I had enough self-induced anesthe-sia, in the form of beer, to take the pain. I was quite evasive with my answers, sometimes turning the answer into a return question. It was amusing to me, and frustrating for them. But soon, I decided that I had had enough.

"Look you guys, if you're looking for me to give you some money, you're wasting your time," I said, telling it as simply as possible.

I took another big swallow of my bud light and wiped away the foam I could feel on my upper lip. I sat and stared at them with a big smile on my face until I had to blow one of those semi-silent burps out the side of my mouth. I could tell they were stunned at my sudden change of mood. I was feeling annoyed and started acting pretty ornery.

"What's your fucking problem all of the sudden?" Chris blurted, his eyes wide.

"Well, Chris, let me tell you my fucking problem." I leaned in closely and added, "I'm sick of everybody trying to dig into my fucking pockets. It happens a lot, and I still haven't figured out why people think they deserve a cut of my inheritance. I just don't get it; I just don't get it. Can you explain to me Chris. Why you think you deserve a cut?"

They both looked at me as if I had just shot their dog. I relished in their amazement. What a couple of morons!

"I just think people who run into a lot of money should help out their friends if they are in need." He told me matter of fact like.

"You're right Chris. I should. And I do. Problem with your and Connie's situation, is you aren't my friends." I told him, mimicking his tone.

It was about at that point, he started getting pretty pissed. It was also about the time that Becky started watching us quite closely. We were obviously getting drunker and drunker. If she had been better at her job, she would have cut us off much sooner, and kicked us out by now. But she didn't, so we continued to make spectacles out of ourselves.

"Hey Becky!" Chris yelled with a slur. "Bring us another pitcher!"

"I'm gonna have to ask you all to leave." The manager informed us calmly.

"Where the hell did you come from? Chris asked, while looking around as if trying to find where this annoying man wearing a tie and a name tag came from. I started to laugh and got up to leave. I was a little unsteady on my feet and grabbed the back of the chair to balance myself. I reached down onto the table and lifted my glass. I raised it in a toast.

"To Connie and Chris! Thanks for a wonderful evening!" With that, I downed the rest of my beer, and set the empty vessel back down with a thud.

"Hey! You're not gonna stick me with the whole check you asshole!" He raged through his drunken stupor.

"I didn't order anything...." I reminded him.

I turned around, one hand still gripping the chair for support. I teetered a bit and headed for the door.

"Fuck you, asshole!" I heard him yell from behind.

I stepped out onto the sidewalk and let the door slam closed behind me. It was dark out now, and kind of chilly. I backed up to the side of the building and leaned on it, trying to clear my head, and figure out a way home.

Good news, in the morning, I woke up in my own bed. I'm not sure how it happened, but I felt lucky and grateful to be there. I also felt extremely hungover, which I deserved. My shoes were off, so I assumed somebody must have helped me. I looked over to the other side of the bed. Boyd was stretched out in his usual spot. I reached over and poked him.

"Boyd? Did you take my shoes off for me last night?" My throat was sore. I must have puked.

CHAPTER 34

JACOB

Doctor Kelley's office seemed particularly claustrophobic as I impatiently waited for her arrival. I wasn't anywhere near in the mood to be there. I was more focused on the million other things I could and should be doing. I could have called and canceled, but I have to pay for the session whether I'm here or not. I'm far too frugal to let something like that happen.

I almost jumped out of my skin when she practically burst through the door. She had an overstuffed shoulder bag draped over her left arm and her laptop clutch underneath her right. A pair of large lens glasses were perched on top of her curly brown perm. Clearly exasperated, she dropped her shit onto the top of the desk.

"Hello! Sorry I'm late." She apologized and exhaled heavily through a lipstick-stained smile.

"Not a problem," I said, smiling back. We went through the usual warmup pleasantries. She seemed a bit distracted, maybe even harried. There were probably things she would rather be doing as well.

After a few more minutes of idle banter, we both settled down a little. I think the realization that we were both stuck there for an hour finally sunk in and we conceded. The whole session ended up consisting of just plain old conversation, as if we were in a coffeehouse, not a doctor's office. Had it not been for the fact that I was paying a lot of money to be there, I probably would have really enjoyed myself.

I was happy to leave the building and carry out my mission for the day. I would be hitting some key businesses along the way home, to buy things for Chuck's coming home party. I was actually pretty excited, I reminded myself of Percy, it made me try and reel myself in. Once I left the Party Store, I realized my purchases were getting awfully heavy. I was too close to home to call an Uber, yet far enough away to take a dreaded shortcut down a strange alley. If it went all the way through, it would come out on the road my apartments on. I would have crossed my fingers, but my hands were full.

That was where fate introduced me to Jacob Livingston. Turns out I could have saved myself a lot of time and trouble by taking the long way home.

* * *

I almost fell when I tripped over Jacob Livingston's ratty tennis shoe. I managed to catch my balance but lost control of a few unsecured shopping bags. His eyes flew open. After a few snorts and a couple of nasty-sounding coughs, he struggled, but made it to his feet. He swayed and staggered as he tried to help me with regrouping my packages.

"I'm terribly sorry. Are you OK?" He stammered a most sincere apology.

"Yes, I'm fine, are you?" I tried to assure him.

He struggled as he tried to help me regroup. His help was more of a hindrance, but I thanked him before continuing down the alley.

It didn't take long before I sensed he was following me. I turned around to confirm my suspicion. He gave me a huge smile, through which I could see his tongue between the gaps in his rotting teeth.

"Say, I hate to ask, but would you happen to have any spare change?" He asked me in a humble tone.

"No, I'm sorry I don't..." I told him regretfully.

I wasn't lying to him. I rarely had any sort of cash on me, only a debit card. His smile faded slightly as he tipped his imaginary hat and walked back to the cardboard mat he had been so rudely awakened on. I don't think either of us had taken more than three steps in the opposite direction before I turned around. I decided to try and buy a ticket to heaven.

My mind went back to Chris. He had told me how he believed people with money should help out those in need. Of course, when he said it, he meant himself, but I decided to take his theory and apply it to this situation.

I led Jacob down the stairs to my apartment. I opened the door and gestured him into my living room. He seemed a bit hesitant as he crossed the threshold, but I gave him a reassuring smile and closed the door behind us. As soon as I heard it click shut, I felt a nauseating wave of hero's remorse. I had never felt it before but instantly identified it, and tried to shake it off. Boyd was on the arm of the couch, he greeted us with his usual cross-eyed stare and a yawn so big that it damn near exposed the entire contents of his head. Jacob placed his plastic Safeway bag of worldly possessions on the floor and wandered toward the cat. He scanned the place with wide eyes as he scratched behind Boyd's very appreciative furry ears.

My first plan of action was to offer Jacob Livingston a nice hot shower. My only fear was that he might decline. I don't think even Boyd could stand his stench for too long. It was a vile combination of body odor, dirty socks, nasty ass, and stale booze. I gave him a grey sweatsuit and one of the unopened toothbrushes I kept stored in the bathroom for unexpected guests. I handed him a clean towel and told him to set his clothes outside the bathroom door.

I picked up the pile of beyond putrid and vomit-invoking clothes. I took them to the laundry while he bathed. I should have burned them.

He emerged from the bathroom and sat at my dining room table. His hair was wet and slicked back on his head. The grey sweats hung loosely on his unusually thin frame. He looked humbled and hungry, but at least he didn't stink anymore. He seemed pretty receptive to the suggestion of a can of Campbell's chicken noodle soup and a ham sandwich on semi-fresh doughy white bread. He ate it like I gave him a time limit. I watched as he gobbled. He made all the cliche noises people make when they enjoy food. His scruffy beard filled quickly with soup juice and breadcrumbs. The experience for me was almost as gratifying as it was disgusting.

Once again, I returned from the laundry, this time with his clothes folded and as clean as they were going to get.

"Thank you so much!" He gushed, as he reached out and accepted them from me.

He disappeared back into the bathroom to change. I had to laugh out loud when he reappeared with his good news.

"They fit again!" He laughed as he tugged at the snug waistband. "It's amazing what a hot dryer and a filling meal can do to one's wardrobe!" We both laughed again.

I offered him a cup of instant coffee and a seat on the sectional. He happily accepted both. The conversation started out a bit slow and slightly awkward, but after a few minutes, I could see he was starting to relax. Boyd took a seat next to the intruder in his regular spot. Jacob stroked the cat's head as he opened up to me. His words began to flow, and I was treated to the Jacob Livingston story.

Life had seemed pretty standard, quintessential all-American middle upper class for Jacob Livingston, up until around 15 years ago. He was a successful accountant, living with his wife Peg and two teenage sons, Mark and Scott, just outside of Spokane. But his emblematic life suddenly blew apart one fateful afternoon.

He had been having a typical day, up until he came home from work. His wife was waiting in the house for him with a request instead of the usual home-cooked meal. She didn't beat around the bush, just flat out asked him for a divorce. She had been seeing the husband half of a couple that had been their close friends since before they were married. Her lover was probably presenting his wife with the same request as they spoke. Jacob said he could feel his heart and his soul both start to disintegrate as she informed him of her plans to leave. He hadn't suspected any problem with their marriage. Which he now admits may have been a problem in itself.

It was just over a week later that Jacob had to be hospitalized. Seems he tried to ace himself with a bottle of cheap vodka, some prescription painkillers, and a bridge that just wasn't quite high enough.

It was after his broken bones healed and his vacation in the padded room was over, that he decided to take a walk. He left the facility and turned east. Home was to the West. He never looked back. He told me he thinks often of his sons. They would both be in their 30s by now. His face had taken on a strangely vacant and glazed look, he had a hint of a tear in the corner of each eye. His voice was strained as he continued.

"I decided to head for Detroit, but never made it past Missoula." He said, staring down at his feet.

"What made you decide to stay in Missoula?" I asked, a bit intrigued.

He lifted his eyes to meet mine.

"Ralph Olson." He stated simply.

Ralph was a political science major with a minor in selling drugs and abusing alcohol. Maybe it was the other way around. Anyway, Ralph was dealing at the time of their chance meeting and invited Jacob to stick around and join in some of the fun. Since he was in no hurry to get to Detroit, and because he wasn't really sure why he was going there anyway, he accepted the invitation. Jacob moved into Ralph's small apartment and lived there for the next seven or eight years. Things were going relatively well, thanks to the lucrative drug scene. They paid the rent on time, ate well, and stayed screwed up pretty much 24/7. They actually considered that success. Jacob said he would probably still be there, hadn't Ralph woke up dead one morning.

Jacob told me the past six or so years have been the worst. He wanders from one place to another on a daily basis, occasionally taking refuge in one of the few homeless facilities in the city, but usually sleeping under bridges. The bulk of his diet consisting of half-eaten fast food from garbage cans outside of the restaurant. Once in a while, a kindhearted person will give him a few bucks or buy him a bag of hot food. Stealing from gardens and fruit trees at night is common in the summer and fall. He said he managed pretty well most of the time, but the winters are always the worst...

I looked like I was still listening, but my thoughts trailed off. One minute I felt sorry for him, and the next, I wanted to smack him upside the head. I wanted to ask him why. Why would he let that unfaithful stupid bitch drive him from his home, career, and two kids? What a weak, pathetic coward he must be. Then suddenly, I would picture him under a bridge sitting on some cardboard in the middle of a below-zero night. I just kept my mouth shut.

I noticed that he had stopped talking. I pulled myself back into the moment; it looked like he did too. We sat silent and sipped our coffee. I heard an unsophisticated slurp before he leaned forward and placed his mug on the scuffed-up coffee table. He rose to his feet and voiced a heartfelt thank you. I watched as he retrieved his plastic grocery store luggage and headed for the door. Instead of letting him leave, like the normal me would have, I asked him to wait. What the hell was going on with me?

I took him downtown and booked him a motel room and paid it up in full for a year. It was a little shit hole, but it was reasonably clean and seemed pretty quiet. I gave him $5000 in cash and a brief lecture full of advice I'm sure he was expecting. He profusely expressed his gratitude. I could see his elation and felt the sincerity of his thank you through his hearty handshake and a spontaneous bear hug.

I decided to keep an eye on him, for no other reason than to see how he was gonna handle his stroke of good luck. I figured one of two things was gonna happen. He would use the money to buy new clothes, get a haircut, and try to resurrect his career... or he would go out and buy drugs and alcohol, sit back, and get fucked up until his rent was due again.

CHAPTER 35

THE HOMECOMING

Percy and I impatiently waited outside of the Missoula airport for Chuck's plane to land. We had jumped the gun a bit and arrived close to an hour early. We sat on a cement bench and people watched, while I chain-smoked and made smart-ass remarks. There was an older couple standing on the curb, obviously waiting for their ride. The woman repeatedly gave me disapproving looks. I could tell she was itching to zap me with the "non-smoking lecture." I continued with my profuse puffing, partly just to irritate her, and partly because it tasted so good. I pretended not to notice her. It was fun to watch her aggravation. She nudged her husband and whispered to him several times. I could tell he was trying to calm her and convince her to mind her own business. He failed.

She turned away from the curb and her husband's disapproval. I watched as she approached with an air of determined confidence. Could she possibly be thinking she had some startling new information on the dangers of smoking? Did she intend on being the one to finally open my eyes with some shocking fact that had eluded me all these years? I smiled as she spoke. Her homily was as expected. The only surprise was a sudden interjection from an unnoticed observer.

An extremely thin, bald man of about 60 years approached our conversation. He nearly stood in between us, as would a referee. He had a pleasant and calm tone as he began his theory, he placed a light and thoughtful hand on each of our shoulders. He turned his attention to the grey-haired woman.

"Madam, please excuse my interruption, but I'm quite sure that this fine young person is well aware of the risks of smoking. I believe your concerns are well intended, but I must point out that the matter is none of your concern." His voice was calm and respectful. Then he turned his attention to me.

"You have the right to smoke, without the judgment of others. I'm sure you know the risks and don't need to be reminded constantly." He patted my shoulder and smiled. I nodded in agreement.

None of this was sitting too well with Mrs. Non-smoker. She moved away slightly to discourage his touch. She huffed back at him.

" Smoking is just another form of suicide!"

His retort was a bit windy, but brilliant. It went a little something like this...

George is at home with a full pack of cigarettes. He decides he wants a bottle of Aquafina. He's mindlessly walking to the corner store. A cat bolts out from across the street, causing a bus to swerve. The bus clips George, throwing him into the air. He lands on the neighbors' picket fence and is impaled. Now George is dead. Why?

Is it the woman that left her slider door open, letting her horny male cat escape to blame?

Is the bus driver at fault for being an animal lover with quick reflexes?

What about the neighbors, for putting up that damn picket fence last year?

Could this whole mess have been avoided if George was a tap water drinker, and had stayed home to smoke a cigarette?

Who can say? One thing is for certain, it wasn't the cigarettes' fault. They were at George's, sitting innocently on the kitchen counter, while the EMTs were loading George's body into the ambulance... My point being, everybody is going to die, no exceptions. God decides when we leave this earth, nobody else. We all need to respect each other and to withhold judgments.

He concluded with another pat on my shoulder. He turned and walked away, back to his pre-intervention location. Grandma grumbled as she shuffled back to the curb. Her husband had the cab door open, waiting for her. I called out behind her.

"It was a pleasure to meet you!" Just before the heavy metal door slammed shut, silencing my sarcasm. They drove out of my life.

I was laughing as I pulled my cell phone out of my pocket. It was just about time for the flight to land. Suddenly and once again, the bald man had a hand on my shoulder. He leaned in close and whispered in my ear.

" I have stage four lung cancer, from a lifetime of smoking." I'm not sure how he did it, but he said it in a cautionary, yet non-judgmental way.

We smiled at each other and again, he walked away. I took one last, hot, nasty drag off my cigarette and snuffed it out into the sand of the conveniently placed ashtray.

I turned my attention to Percy, He was studying his phone, oblivious to his surroundings.

"Percy! It's showtime, let's head for the gate." I said with a wave toward the entrance.

He looked up and smiled as he rose off the bench.

"Oh, I'm so excited!" He squealed before doing a little skip and heading for the glass doors.

We walked toward the gates, pausing momentarily to gawk at the gigantic stuffed grizzly bear displayed by a waiting area.

"Oh, how sad, poor care bear!" He said through an exaggerated frown.

I rolled my eyes and tugged his sleeve, indicating that he should follow me to the gate.

"What were you talking to those old people about?" Percy asked me out of the blue.

"Oh nothing, just passing time with idle bullshit," I said smiling at him.

Percy clapped and waved as he watched Chuck descend the escalator, Chuck reciprocated in kind. I could feel the ridiculous smile plastered on my face as he approached. After a hug or two, we went to baggage claim and collected his luggage, then went outside and climbed into the waiting cab. Chuck was surprised, to say the least, when we pulled into Johnny Carino's parking lot instead of heading for home.

We had reserved a whole section of the restaurant for the big homecoming bash. There were in excess of 30 people in attendance. Mostly Chuck's fag friends, many of which had a huge hand in the planning and decorating of the whole event. You can imagine how beautiful it was. The only truly tawdry thing in the room was the penis-shaped cake, courtesy of Percy's nemesis, Aaron. It was red velvet, iced with cream cheese frosting, and filled with Bavarian cream. The toasted coconut was used for pubic hair. I didn't have any.

Chuck was surprised and overly delighted to see such a large crowd there just to honor him. He clapped, squealed with laughter, and instantaneously assumed his Liberace persona.

"For me?! Oh my God! Thank you so much everybody!" He gushed; his chubby hands folded against his heart.

Everybody clapped for him, and somebody started singing "for he's a jolly good fellow", and everybody joined in. Chuck was beaming. The whole evening was nothing short of fabulous. I loved watching Chuck in full blown celebratory action. Aaron assembled most of the guest list because Chuck and I don't share many mutual friends, with the exception of Percy. But as we all know, there was no way Percy was going to work alongside Aaron. He was such a baby.

I saw a lot of people that I hadn't seen since that fateful New Year's Eve party... the horrifically eventful night that led to this bittersweet occasion. That realization was a little jarring, but it reminded me of Chuck's incredible mental tenacity.

I woke up around 11:00 AM the next morning. Once again, I had no idea how I got there. I lay there for a minute thinking about how irresponsible I've become. I was gonna have to work on that.

I swung my legs over the side of the bed and sat up. I instantly knew that I was still pretty drunk. I decided to sit there for a little while and gather my bearings. Boyd suddenly jumped up and put his paws on my shoulders, then head-butted me. I don't think he liked that I hadn't fed him breakfast at his usual 9:00 o'clock. I got the hint and stood up. Thank God for bedposts, or I would have hit the floor.

Once I finally made it to the kitchen, I filled up a tumbler with ice and water. I drank it down and filled it again... and again. Meanwhile, Boyd was rubbing against my legs, and pushing his weight against me. I had to hold on to the edge of the counter to keep from falling down. It was ridiculous.

Ever tried opening a can of cat food with one hand? It wasn't easy, but we gotta do what we gotta do. I got pretty dizzy leaning over to set it on the floor for him. He started gobbling it up, so I headed back for the bedroom.

I staggered to the edge of the bed, then remembered I had to pee really bad. I held onto the footboard as long as I could, then had to take a stumble of faith towards the door and grab the knob. Success... I made it, and I was still on my feet.

I turned the knob and pushed the door open. Then I froze. Talk about an early morning assault on the eyes! Chuck was stark naked, passed out, and completely engulfing the toilet with his huge doughy white mass. His appallingly exposed ass was sticking up in the air, supported by his bent knees. Puke was everywhere, it covered the back of the tank, the surrounding floor, and the bottom half of the shower curtain. I gagged. I grabbed the towel that was hanging from the rack and covered my nose and mouth with it. I crept forward just enough so that I could reach him with my foot. I lifted it and gave a quick but firm push to the thigh. He groaned in protest.

" Sorry, just checking to see if you're alive..." I said in a semi whisper.

I guess the real shocker was when I noticed the little Asian guy sleeping in the bathtub. He was partially naked, wearing nothing but a hot-pink cropped T-shirt and a pair of women's floral-patterned booty socks. What the hell?

I knew there was no way I would make it up the stairs, in my condition, to Chuck's apartment. I ended up peeing in a coffee can and dumping it outside. Not one of my finer moments. But we do, what we gotta do. Right?

CHAPTER 36

A FALL FROM GRACE

I've come to think of Doctor Kelley as somewhat of a friend, kind of easing out of the acquaintance category. Although, I could be mistaken, normally you don't have to pay your friends to talk to you. I guess you could say she's in a class all by herself, in a newly created category. I could call it "prostitute- friend-like-acquaintances." I think the payment element in the relationship is what gives me the confidence to believe that she is being honest. Voluntary friends can sometimes tell you what you want to hear to spare your feelings. I guess they both have their place, depending on what you are looking for at the moment

I decided to tell her about finding Chuck in the bathroom, the morning after his welcome home party. Anytime I tell her a Chuck tale, she tries not to look aghast, usually quite unsuccessfully. Seems this particular session, Doctor Kelley was ready to speak her mind. She wasn't trying to hide her expressions or opinions, like a good prostitute- friend-like-acquaintance should. I finished the story and sat watching her, waiting for her reaction.

She raised her eyebrows and cocked her head, the way you would say "really?", without actually using your voice. She stood up from her desk and tapped the tips of her fingers on its surface. She walked over to a half-dead spider plant sitting on the dusty bookcase and began plucking off shriveled leaves. It was obvious that she was pondering, maybe looking for the appropriate words. After the brief foliage grooming, she returned to her desk, sat, and pulled the chair in as close as her body would allow. Then the hands folded... I was in for it.

She didn't beat around the bush.

"Chuck's nothing more than a ticking time bomb. Not just to himself, but to your relationship with him." She stated matter of factly.

I instantly felt defensive. I knew what she meant about his lifestyle. Yes, he was reckless. But what about the other part? I think she took my furrowed eyebrows as a cue to explain.

"Chuck has a best friend, and you don't... to put it simply." She said, then leaned back in her chair.

She brought her point home pretty clearly through a series of examples. I can't tell you how surprised I was at the shocking realization that she was right.

What was I supposed to do with this information? I asked myself. Apparently, she can read minds.

She plucked a pencil from an overstuffed holder and began taping it on the desk protector. After a few seconds, she stopped and pointed it, eraser first, straight at me.

"Sometimes we're better off without certain people in our lives." She shrugged as she advised.

"So, what do you suggest?" I snapped. "Are you saying I should go home and tell Chuck to fuck off?!" My voice full of rage and disbelief.

"Please calm down." She said in a soothing tone, which pissed me off even more.

Maybe she was giving me good advice, but I had to dismiss it. I think I'm gonna move her all the way back into the acquaintance category.

CHAPTER 37

NOW WHAT?

My face was engulfed in a cloud of steam billowing from the pot of boiling elbow macaroni. I was stirring away, and patiently waiting to drain it and add that big clump of greasy butter and mix in that little envelope of neon orange powder. I can't remember the last time I enjoyed the goodness of a box of Kraft Mac'n cheese. Normally, I end up putting a halt to its preparation when I remember that it requires a small amount of effort and roughly 10 minutes of my time. Cup-O-noodles usually wins out, requiring no effort, and about 3 minutes in the microwave, plus you eat it right out of the container.

I didn't bother with a bowl. I grabbed a fork and took the entire pan into the living room, sat on the couch and turned on the TV. I got one big bite shoveled into my mouth before the phone rang. It was my mom.

I had a sinking feeling the moment she began to speak. She sounded strange. I braced myself. She went through the usual pleasantries that eventually led up to the real reason for the call.

"What's going on mom?" I cut in on her, getting sick of her procrastination. She paused before answering, as if finding it difficult to say the words.

"Kyle died last night." She barely could get the words out through the sudden sobs.

She and dad were heading for Joy's place right away, and suggested I do the same. I hung up the phone and went straight for the closet containing my crusty old suitcase. I left some money on the counter for Chuck in case I ran out of anything. He said he would stay in my apartment with Boyd until I got back.

I took a cab from the airport to the location of Joy's partially constructed dream home. She and Kyle had been living in a rented motorhome on-site, while waiting for its completion. I paid the driver and got out, grabbed my suitcase, and headed toward Joy's temporary residence. She was sitting on the foldout step of the huge vehicle. She seemed small and defeated. She looked in my direction, and a slow but sincere smile came over her face. She stood up and headed towards me. As we grew closer both of us extended our arms. We embraced and said nothing; we just held each other and cried. I will never forget that moment.

Inside the motorhome, we sat at a small collapsible table and talked. I let her lead; I only wanted her to share what she was ready to and comfortable with.

Despite the melancholy mood, we enjoyed the evening together. We went outside and sat at the picnic table, grilled a couple of steaks, and shared a bottle of red wine. She gave me a tour of her yet to be completed home; It was shaping up to be quite a place. We took a long walk and talked till late into the night. Mom and dad arrived early the next morning. We spent the day completing arrangements and tying up loose ends. It was nice to see mom and dad, and Joy seemed to take comfort in them being there.

The service was beautiful. That's what everyone told us. I guess I just didn't see the beauty in it. My sister sat on a pew sobbing at the loss of her best friend and beloved husband. The whole scenario was quite ugly if you ask me. I don't think there was a soul in attendance that didn't tell Joy that Kyle was now in a better place. Somehow, I think she disagreed.

I arrived home late in the afternoon. The moment I stepped in the door, Boyd came running. I dropped my suitcase and bent down to pick him up. I carried him with me into the kitchen to grab the cold beer I knew was waiting for me. I twisted the top off of the chilly bottle and tipped it back. During my lengthy swig, I caught a peripheral glimpse of the mac and cheese pan. It only took a few seconds for me to realize that it was empty, actually clean. I sat my half-empty bottle on the counter and placed Boyd back on the floor. I picked up the pot to inspect it closer. Boyd's loud meow drew my attention to the floor. He rubbed up against my leg and then trotted towards his feeding station. Both his food dish and water bowl were empty. What the hell? I went into the bathroom to find his litter box overflowing; the stench made my eyes water. The toilet lid was up, and the seat was covered in cat prints and loose kitty gravel. Apparently, in a pinch, cats can survive for a week on toilet water and dried-up Kraft macaroni and cheese. I decided to clean things up and feed

Boyd before ascending the stairs to Chuck's apartment to find out what the fuck was going on.

CHAPTER 38

A LOT OF BITTERSWEET

Doctor Kelley was busy rifling through a thick stack of papers on her desk as I entered the room. I hesitated at the door for a moment when I realized she hadn't noticed I was there. Beyond her silhouette was the couch, glowing in the sunlight that filtered through the dirty windows behind it. It was in that moment that I realized it wasn't such a mystery as to why I kept coming here. It always had a feeling of familiarity, a real consistency. For the short periods of time I spent there, I felt safe. It was like a hiding place, maybe even a sanctuary of sorts.

As I walked past her desk, I gave it an attention-seeking tap with my fingers. She looked up with a huge smile on her face. I could tell she had been thinking about something happy before I walked in. I took my usual position on the semi-new tan suede. She folded her hands and rested them on the partially read stack of papers; she was practically glowing.

"Something seems to have you in a pretty good mood today?" I mentioned, with an air of question in my voice.

Her smile widened as she lifted her left hand in my direction. There was a gold band with a solitary diamond wrapped around her fourth finger.

"I now have a fiancé." She gushed, as calmly as possible.

"That's wonderful, congratulations!" I told her, in all sincerity. I was truly happy for her. It made me wonder if I was maturing a little bit...

We sat silent for a moment, both looking at the small but beautiful ring. Then, like a sudden interruption, I felt my reality creep up. I could feel my smile fade slowly as my head fell slightly to the left; maybe because that's the side the heart is on. I saw her eyes darken as she analyzed my body language. It was time to tell her what had happened three days before.

* * *

I scaled up the stairs to Chuck's apartment, the way somebody actually in shape would. It's amazing how blind rage can turn you bionic. Before I knew it, I was pounding wildly on his door.

"Chuck?! Open the god damn door!" I demanded.

I was interrupted by Ruth, the semi-reclusive woman in the neighboring apartment.

"Stop that banging! He's not home! Guess he must have got sick; the ambulance took him away a few days back!" She stood looking at me for a moment before she shrugged her shoulders and disappeared back into her apartment.

I ran back downstairs and frantically searched for my cell

phone. As I was searching, it dawned on me that I hadn't used it since I left for California. I rarely received calls, and next to never made them, so it didn't seem strange until that moment. We were far too busy down South planning and attending a funeral to worry about anything else. I guess I knew in my heart that if something was wrong, Chuck would get ahold of me. My hands were shaking as I inspected the phone, hoping to see a text or missed call. It was dead. I ran into my bedroom to find my charger still plugged in next to the lamp, I had forgotten to take it with me, not that I would have used it anyway, apparently. Because of my nervousness, I had a hard time getting the phone plugged in. I paced around the apartment, waiting for it to charge enough so that I could call a cab or an Uber. It seemed like an eternity before I was stepping into my ride.

I walked into Chuck's room to find him startlingly pale. He was hooked up to a few different machines which made pumping and hissing sounds. It was odd how small he looked. Percy was sitting in what looked like a conference room chair, butted up as close to the bed as possible. He too, was as white as a sheet. They both smiled when they saw me. Chuck raised a heavy and slow hand to pull his oxygen mask off to one side.

"What, no flowers?" His voice was low and breathy, yet still had his signature sarcastic humor.

"Sorry, I was in a bit of a rush to get here," I told him as I walked toward the bed.

"I'll forgive you this time."

"Thanks, I won't let it happen again," I promised while making a cross over my heart.

He gave a slight nod and slid the oxygen mask back into

place, his hand falling limply back to the bed. I kept smiling, despite my sudden urge to gasp. He closed his eyes and was instantly asleep. Percy suggested with a whisper that we should chat in the cafeteria.

We each took a seat across from one another and began pouring multiple sugar packets into lukewarm and very bitter coffee. I sat silent and allowed Percy to frantically purge the details of the past week through tears and multiple Kleenex.

It began with a spontaneous visit to Chuck's place close to a week earlier. He had stopped at McDonald's and bought a bag full of what he calls goodies, including Chuck's beloved chicken nuggets. He said he loved to surprise Chuck by doing things like that. As it turned out, Percy was the one surprised.

He said he was concerned from the moment he reached Chuck's door. It was ajar, which was unusual. Chuck usually kept his door locked, even when he was home. He said he pushed open the door slowly.

"Chuck?" He called as he poked his head in the apartment. "Are you home? I've brought us some lunch...." With that, he stepped in and shut the door behind him.

"Oh my God!" He screamed and dropped the loaded bag onto the floor.

Chuck was on the sofa, obviously writhing in pain. He had his knees pulled up as high as he could, his arms wrapped tightly around them, and was shivering and crying. His face was a strange shade of grey, and his eyes were blood red, when he looked up at Percy.

"Help me Percy. I'm so cold." He stammered as he struggled to get the words out.

Percy fell to his knees beside his friend and managed to dial 911.

It seemed Chuck felt the need to hide the fact that his surgical wounds had become infected some time ago. He had been trying to medicate himself with over-the-counter treatments and failed miserably. Because of the lack of proper treatment, he developed sepsis. Percy explained that this meant his blood had become infected. I could feel the color drain from my face, and I was suddenly lightheaded. Then he told me Chuck had been hiding another secret. He was a type 2 diabetic, which complicated things even more. I felt the sting of my coffee racing into my throat. I took a deep breath, and fought it back down. I tried to keep a calm expression. I didn't want Percy to see my growing panic.

We made our way back to Chuck's room and entered quietly. He still looked small and pale, like he had 30 some minutes ago, only now he was sitting up. Percy resumed his position in the chair beside the bed. I could tell Chuck was trying to appear lucid, but he wasn't doing a very good job. He was having trouble concentrating and seemed to be struggling to stay awake. I was having a hard time concealing my escalating alarm.

A young Asian doctor wearing green scrubs and clutching a clipboard asked Percy and I out into the hallway. We stood and watched him as he studied the attached paperwork for a moment or two.

"This is the situation thus far. Chuck's white blood count is through the roof, and his blood pressure is dangerously low." Percy yelped and clasped his hand over his mouth, interrupting him. "The intravenous antibiotic drip he's being administered isn't proving effective. So, we decided we're going to change things up a bit and see how that goes. If it's successful, we should see immediate results." He studied the paper a few more seconds and walked away without looking up.

He wasn't the most personable doctor I had ever met, but I was glad to hear they were gonna try something else. Percy stood weeping.

"Come on Percy, get it together," I told him in a firm yet gentle voice.

"I know, I'm sorry, I just can't help it! I'm so worried!" He explained while wiping tears from his eyes onto his pants.

"I know, me too, but we don't want Chuck to see us scared. Do you think you can do that? I encouraged him with a whisper.

"Yeah, yeah, I can." He said through a smile and a reassuring nod.

I looked at him and used my index fingers to push the corners of my mouth up, reminding him to smile as we headed for the door. We went back in and assumed our earlier positions.

Our very sick friend was asleep, so we just took our seats. We sat quietly most of the time. Every now and then, he would wake up for a few minutes, so we made sure that one of us was always in the room, for fear of missing one of those occasions. It was one of the longest and most stressful days of my life.

Early evening rolled around, and we were handed a new ray of hope. Chuck woke up and seemed much more alert. His face even looked like it had regained some of its color, and he said he was hungry for something actually edible. I guess he wasn't that fond of the hospital cuisine.

"Are you allowed to eat food from outside the hospital?" Percy asked him cautiously.

"I'm sure they won't mind as long as you don't tell them." He winked at Percy. "There's a Wendy's just down the road." He informed, before even being asked what he would like.

"I'll be back as quick as I can!" With that, Percy grabbed his coat and headed out the door.

"Thank you, doll!" Chuck called after Percy, still sounding a bit weak. He turned his attention to me.

"Is Boyd OK?" His eyes were full of concern.

"Don't worry, he's just fine. But I don't think he's gonna wanna have macaroni and cheese again anytime soon." I told him through a laugh.

I could tell he was relieved. He smiled briefly. Then the concerned look made a comeback.

"Did everything go OK at your sister's?"

"Yeah, everything went fine, it's gonna take her a while to get used to Kyle being gone, but she's gonna be OK." The news made his smile return.

It felt good to be sitting next to him.

"Good afternoon." Dr. Chien announced as he walked into the room.

"I'm here to give you a little checkup, Chuck." He informed, then directed his attention to me. "Do you mind giving us a little privacy for a few minutes?" I patted Chuck on the knee before getting up and leaving the room.

I was sitting outside in the hallway when the elevator doors opened, and Percy stepped out holding two large takeout bags. He held them up in the air and smiled as he walked over to me.

"I went through Wendy's and McDonald's!" His tone was giddy.

"We need to wait out here for a bit. The doctor is giving Chuck another once over."

"Should I hide these bags?" Percy asked, slightly alarmed.

"Nah, if he asks, we'll say they are just for us," I said, hoping to remove his worry.

"Oh, that's a good idea." He smiled, not sounding all that confident in my plan.

A few minutes later, Doctor Chien walked out of the room. He stopped and talked to us briefly, explaining that Chuck was showing significant improvement. I can't begin to express the relief I felt, and by the look on Percy's face, he was feeling the same.

"You two enjoy your dinner. The nurse will be bringing up a tray for Chuck shortly." He winked at us before he walked away, obviously knowing full well that it was a dinner for three.

Chuck was smiling as we walked back into the room.

"I'm doing way better!" He sang in a mock falsetto voice. Percy clapped enthusiastically, while performing a small Irish jig.

I was smiling from ear to ear as I walked over to Chuck's bedside and handed him the two bags full of greasy delights. He let out a little squeal of anticipation as he rifled through the bags in search of the Chicken McNuggets.

We spent the rest of the evening as if we were in my living room, minus the alcohol, and an oversized Siamese cat.

We skipped around the channels but watched mostly HGTV shows. Chuck's particularly fond of Love it or List it. I told him that I had set the DVR to record "The Young and the Restless" so that he could catch up when he gets out of the hospital. He was having a really good night... Then nurse Ratchet came in.

"Sorry folks, visiting hours are over!" She announced with no-nonsense in her voice.

"Oh phooey! Just a few more minutes, OK?" Chuck pleaded, as if he were eight years old, begging his mother.

"Sorry Chuck, hospital policy." She smiled; it was directed at me.

I'm not sure of the logistics of the arrangement, but Percy was allowed to stay overnight. And I was quite happy about it.

"OK, OK, I can take a hint!" I told her as I stood up to leave.

I grabbed my coat and my cell phone. I called for a cab, then walked back over to Chuck.

" I'll come back in the morning, Chuck." Then I leaned over and surprised myself by kissing the top of his head. "I'll apologize to Boyd for you," I said jokingly, hoping to suppress my emotion.

He reached up and squeezed my hand. "Yes, please do that for me." His eye welled up with tears. I turned away and walked toward the door. I grabbed the handle and pulled it open. I turned back and gave a little wave to Percy and shot Chuck a reassuring smile. The door floated close behind me, and I stood there for a minute. I felt so much gratitude... My friend was gonna be OK.

I was pretty tired by the time I got home. On my way to the bedroom, I topped off Boyd's water and refilled his Tony the Tiger bowl and apologized to him for Chuck. I barely made it through the thankful prayer I was saying before I fell asleep.

As fond of McDonald's as Chucky is, he didn't really care for the breakfast menu, so I ordered three vanilla lattes instead. It was around 7:00 AM when I entered Chuck's room the next morning. I sat the three freshly bought coffees on the small table just inside the door. Damn, they were hot. I looked up with an enthusiastic smile and suddenly froze.

Percy was sitting exactly where he was when I left the evening before, only now the bed next to him was empty. He had an almost blank expression on his face, tinged slightly with disbelief. I tried not to panic.

"What's going on? Where's Chuck?" Restraining my voice from screaming.

He didn't answer me. He just looked at me with red-rimmed eyes.

"God damn it, Percy! Where's Chuck?!" I demanded, this time with much less control.

"He's gone," He told me, in a barely audible whisper.

"What the fuck do you mean he's gone?!" I screamed at him and grabbed his shoulders.

I started shaking him and demanding answers. His sobs became uncontrollable.

"He's dead!" He screamed in my face.

I let my arms fall to my sides. I stared into his eyes, unable to speak. I already knew what had happened, but hearing the words stunned me to my soul. I staggered over to the nearest chair and collapsed into it. My face fell into my hands and remained there while I tried to collect myself. My tears ran through my fingers and landed on the floor between my feet.

CHAPTER 39

A BIG LAST DAY

Chuck's mom had his body sent to Seattle to be buried next to his father. I followed. I arrived at the cemetery in time to find an extremely large crowd already in attendance. It looked like there were just slightly more fags and drag queens than 60 plus conservative middle-class Christians. Everyone seemed quite at peace with one another, I guess they would. They all knew Chuck.

We were signaled that it was time. A procession of cars full of mixed mourners drove down the inner cemetery road to the site of Chuck's service. It kind of looked like an outdoor theater, partially covered. I remember thinking how fortunate we were to have decent weather that day. Typically, in Seattle, half of us would be getting wet.

There was a lot of muted chatter as everyone found his or her seat. Chuck's mom invited me to join her and assorted aunts, uncles and cousins of Chuck's in the front row. I politely declined, I wanted to hang back a bit. A short, chubby man with very red cheeks and a white-collar appeared behind the permanent wooden pulpit. His sudden presence hushed the crowd. He delivered a traditional, generic, and predictable service. At the end, he asked us all to bow our heads in prayer, after which he asked if there was anybody in attendance that would like to say a few words. I was amazed at the number of arms that shot up in the air. People took turns telling stories of experiences they shared with Chuck. They triggered tidal waves of alternating laughter and tears. Seattle was likely to see a Kleenex shortage in the morning. I realized that there were probably more people at his funeral than I knew collectively. During another visual pass, Percy caught my eye. He was crying and clutching the arm of a tall, thin, young man wearing a yellow high neck sweater and a pink pencil skirt. I must admit, the sight made me chuckle to myself.

Father Greg instructed us to proceed to the burial site. We walked in complete silence, apart from heavy footsteps, to place Chuck where he would spend eternity. I could see the casket in the distance. It was suspended with poles over a precise hole, waiting to be lowered down. It made my skin crawl. We reached the gravesite, and everyone gathered around it. Chuck was gone, and this was what we were going to do with him. I wanted to scream. This was the first time I ever stood alone, in a crowd.

The box holding my friend was slowly being lowered into the ground. I could barely stand the thought of him being covered in six feet of cold, wet dirt and rocks. I stood and imagined myself living every day for the rest of my life with that haunting image. He should have been cremated. That way he could have stayed with Boyd and me in our apartment, where he would be warm and dry. I knew I wasn't thinking rationally. It was only Chuck's shell in that box. I hoped to God that the real Chuck was above us, looking down and digging all the attention. But my mourning and disbelief kept leading me down darker paths.

I stood silently with my head hanging low; anyone who may have looked my way might have thought I was praying. But I was actually just trying to hide from the moment. It just might have worked, hadn't I suddenly felt a hand on my shoulder. The touch caused me to raise my head and open my eyes, just in time to see the top of the casket disappear under the horizon of the earth. I turned to see who had interrupted my denial. It was Percy. His eyes were red and swollen and he seemed even smaller than usual. I wanted to take comfort in his presence, but I didn't, or couldn't, at least not for now. In that moment, there really wasn't a Percy without a Chuck. I offered a weak smile before looking away.

I stood and waited until every last mourner had gone. A light rain began to fall, and a crew had come to cover Chuck with dirt. As I watched, I wanted to call them obscene names, to tell them to stop it! I was still there when they left.

CHAPTER 40

KENNY DUNN

Doctor Kelley was running late. I sat in her office, in my familiar spot on the couch, and stared at the wall. Any other day I wouldn't have minded, but I really felt like talking to her this time, I needed to. I wasn't sure what I was going to say exactly, but it felt urgent. Half of me wanted to spew everything in my mind; the other half didn't want to talk at all. I don't remember a time before that day that I actually felt like a patient in need of this service.

I felt a surge of relief when I heard the door open. My body involuntarily sat up straight, in full attention. It seemed like it took her forever to sit down and get situated. Once she had her hands folded on her desk and was focused on me, I drew a blank.

"Is everything OK with you today?" She asked me, her brow furrowed in question. "You seem upset about something."

I was. I told her pretty much every detail of the funeral. I shared feelings with her that I wasn't even aware I had. But it all boiled down to how I was going to cope with my biggest and most disturbing obsession.

"Doctor Kelley, I don't know how I'm gonna cope with Chuck being buried." It came out as if I was pleading for help. I hadn't planned on sounding that desperate.

"I keep picturing him, laying in that box 6 feet under all that dirt. I think of the cold and the wet. I dream about him rotting away, and I wake up practically screaming. I can't get away from it, I don't know what to do!" I began to sob and covered my face with my hands.

I think that if she ever questioned my mental stability before, I solidified her suspicions today.

"Have you ever felt this way before? After other funerals?" She asked. Her voice was gentle.

"Actually, yes. I felt a lot like this when my grandpa died, but somehow this is worse, way worse." I choked back another urge to sob.

I told her that after grandpa's funeral, I knew that I wanted to be cremated. I made my decision clear to my family. I hope they were listening to me. I didn't want anybody throwing my ass, dead or alive, into any fucking hole and covering me with dirt, then walking away.

With that being said, my mind suddenly went back to a story grandpa had told me back when I was way too young to hear it. It could very well be the root of my fears today. I felt a look of repulsion take over my face. Doctor Kelley noticed it and furrowed her eyebrows in question again. I decided to share the story of grandpa's childhood friend, Kenny Dunn with her.

* * *

My grandpa on my mom's side, Carl, told me that he and his friend Kenny would go fishing every Saturday morning, rain or shine. They rarely caught anything, but always had a lot of fun. Kenny was a short, skinny kid with sandy blonde hair that hung in his eyes most of the time, and his clothes were always dirty and worn. But his spirits were always high, and he was quite the jokester, even in school. His mom was a small, pretty blonde lady and was very kind; she always welcomed gramps into her home. After fishing, they looked forward to the honey sandwiches on white bread she would never fail to provide at lunchtime.

One Saturday wasn't quite as Norman Rockwell as all the previous...

The two young boys sat on the steps of Kenny Dunn's decaying house, which sat at the end of a long, dirt driveway, just off the road leading out of town. They exchanged jokes and jabs while licking stray honey from their fingers. The sun shone bright that day and lit up the trees surrounding the Dunn family farm. Next to the house was a barn covered in a coat of badly peeling red paint. Chickens and barn cats walked freely about; it seemed like the most peaceful place on earth and the perfect playground for two little schoolboys.

The crack and rumble of a distant shotgun blast ripped through the afternoon air, distracting them only momentarily. Everybody had rifles in the area, and the noise became commonplace.

The rickety screen door behind them swung open with

the sound of screeching hinges. Mrs. Dunn stood holding out a coin.

"Kenny, I need you to walk up to the grocery and bring me back a small sack of sugar."

Kenny jumped to his feet and took the coin from his mom. "Let's go, Carl!" He exclaimed excitedly to his friend. They had a mission.

They took off down the driveway. The dry dirt below their feet billowed like smoke behind them as they ran.

"Don't doddle!" They could hear Mrs. Dunn call from behind.

They spotted Kenny's dad up ahead. He seemed to be walking quite fast and headed straight towards them. They slowed to a walk as they tried to catch their breaths. The elder Dunn was almost upon them.

"Hi dad!" Kenny said and waved his hand in a cheerful greeting.

His dad didn't answer. He just grabbed Kenny by the collar and started pulling him back in the direction of the house. Grandpa said he went against his better judgment and followed them when he should have been running for home.

They reached the front steps of the porch. Kenny's dad released his collar and shoved him to the dirt.

"Don't you go anywhere, boy!" He warned, his face red with rage. He stomped like a madman up to the door and went inside, slamming it behind him.

Kenny stood looking at the door in disbelief. It was the first time he had ever seen his dad like this. The boys sat back down on the steps; in the same spots, they were in before the world suddenly changed.

Carl could feel Kenny's embarrassment and confusion. They sat silent and uncomfortable until they heard the sound of a faint whimper. They looked up to see Kenny's dog, Maxi, dragging herself along the ground towards the house. Before they could even get to their feet, Kenny's dad was out the door and practically flew past them. He grabbed Maxi by the collar and drugged her limp, bloodied body around the side of the house. Kenny let out a truly blood-curdling scream. He jumped up and ran after them.

Carl rounded the corner to find Mr. Dunn frantically digging a hole. Kenny was clinging to his arm, pulling on it with all his might, in an attempt to stop him. His dad knocked him to the ground several times and continued his task at a frantic pace.

Suddenly, Mrs. Dunn appeared screaming hysterically.

"What in the world is going on!" She grabbed at the shovel. "John! Stop it now!" She demanded.

He stopped and stood, breathing hard. His nostrils flared, and his eyes were wild. He raised the shovel high above his shoulder and swung it hard, hitting his wife on the side of the head, sending her to the ground with a heavy thud. While he had the chance, Carl ran around the house and crawled under the porch.

Kenny lay on the ground crying frantically and screaming for his mother. He tried crawling to her but was stopped by his shovel-wielding father. Both he and his mom were motionless during the rest of the tragedy.

Carl watched helplessly from underneath the porch. Mr. Dunn continued to grunt, sweat and curse his way through the hard dry soil. When he was finally satisfied with graves depth, he threw the shovel to the ground and practically lunged for the dog. He jerked her up by the collar and raised her up in front of his face. She dangled in front of him like a prized 30-pound salmon. He carried her over to the hole and screamed in her face.

"Nobody kills chickens on this farm except for me!" He threw poor Maxi into the pit with brute force, enough to make the half-dead dog scream.

Carl had to cover his mouth to keep from crying out. John grabbed the shovel and preceded to replace the dirt. When he finished, he stomped it down with his heavy boots. Once again, he threw down the shovel. He looked at his motionless family and spat on the ground before he headed back into the house. Carl ran as fast as he could down the dry dirt driveway for home, leaving quite a dust plume in his wake.

When grandpa arrived home, He told his parents what happened. They called the police. Miraculously, Kenny and his mom recovered... at least physically. Mr. Dunn spent over a year in prison, after which time his wife allowed him to come home. (Grandpa said the shovel to the head must have really knocked something loose in her brain for her to even consider letting him come back.)

Grandpa explained that when Kenny finally came back to school, he wasn't the same kid. He didn't joke around anymore or talk much at all. Their Saturday morning fishing trips ceased with their friendship. As the years went by, grandpa said Kenny all but disappeared. He hadn't gone anywhere, he had become a recluse, and nobody really noticed him anymore, until one day.

George Mason burst into the quiet classroom filled with all

16 of the town's high school seniors. He announced, almost eagerly, that Kenny Dunn had been arrested. George's father was the town sheriff, allowing him first-hand information. Seems Kenny killed his father and cut him up into several pieces. Then he walked to the police station and delivered a full confession along with a bag of gruesome evidence. He told the deputy that his dad was butchering a deer in the barn. He was supposed to help but instead saw it as the opportunity he had been waiting for most of his life.

They asked him why he took the time and effort to chop him up. He told them that as much as he hated his father, he wanted to make sure that he wasn't buried alive.

Thanks gramps.

CHAPTER 41

JUST DO IT

I had a job to do, and I was pretty sure it was going to be the hardest one of my life. Chuck's mom had asked if I would take care of his apartment. She said she couldn't bear the thought of going through her only son's possessions, much less getting rid of them. I wanted to tell her that I didn't think the task would be much easier for me, but instead, I told her I would be happy to do it. I was pretty sure her pain was even deeper than mine, and if that were the case, she would be completely incapable of performing it herself. She told me there were a few things that she wanted to keep, and would I send them to her. I told her I would. I paid Chuck's rent for another month; I just wasn't ready to do it yet.

It was down to the last week when I decided to just do it. Against my better judgment, I called Percy.

I waited outside Chuck's door for what seemed like an eternity. I couldn't bring myself to go inside alone, so I waited for the ever-tardy Percy to arrive. His car screeched to a stop.

He jumped out and was instantly ascending the stairs two at a time, spewing apologies all the way to the top. We stood for a moment as he caught his breath.

"I'm so sorry I'm late!" He leaned over, placing his hands on his knees and resting.

"It's OK Percy, it's not like I'm excited to get started," I said half-jokingly.

He stood upright and nodded slightly in agreement.

I inserted the key and reluctantly turned it. A small half-hearted shove followed, and the door creaked forward enough to let out a hint of stale air. Percy took a huge breath and exhaled what seemed like a gale storm. He looked at me with a question in his eyes.

"Are we ready for this?" He asked hesitantly.

"No..." I told him, then he pushed the door the rest of the way open.

We hesitated before crossing the threshold. It surprised me that he stepped in first. I followed.

It was as if we stepped into a moment that had been frozen in time. The McDonald's bag holding Chuck's beloved chicken nuggets lay on the floor where they landed on his fateful last day at home. Percy gasped at the sight of it. He practically lunged at it, grabbing the petrified package and clutching it tightly against his chest. He began sobbing uncontrollably, reminding me of why I was so reluctant to invite him. I guess being there alone was the only worse thing. I pried the stale bag from his grip and took it promptly to the kitchen trash.

"No, please!" He wailed as he followed me.

I dropped the bag in the can and replaced the lid.

"Knock it off Percy, pull yourself together! It's garbage! What did you wanna do? Press the whole thing into a scrapbook?!" I snapped at him with impatience.

He let out a series of sobs as he clutched his head. Somebody was going to have to buck up here, and it looked like it was gonna have to be me.

I decided to start in the bedroom. His bed was unmade. I pictured him getting out of that spot for the last time. Suddenly I was choking back a wave of emotion. I actually had to hold myself back from smelling his pillow, which would have been way too cliché. The thought made me laugh quietly. Percy entered the room; he seemed to have collected himself enough to be instructed. We were gonna get this done. I gave him a verbal list of the items Chuck's mom had requested. It was going to be his job to collect them. He agreed to his assignment and left the room. I knew of only one keepsake I wanted for myself. It was a picture Chuck had framed and displayed on his dresser. It was a picture of Boyd and me last Christmas; we had taped a bow on the poor cat's head. I struggled to keep him from shaking it off before Chuck could snap the photo. It was rare for Chuck to possess a shot that he wasn't in, much less showcase it, so I knew it must have meant a lot to him.

The day dragged on as we tackled chore after chore. The Salvation Army was going to pick everything up in the morning. The last thing we did was pack up Chuck's clothes. Percy thought they should go to the men's shelter.

"I don't know Percy... how many gay men do you think are walking around Missoula with 48-inch waists?" We laughed.

CHAPTER 42

FAREWELL DR. KELLEY

I walked into the welcome familiarity of Doctor Kelley's office right on time. She was at her desk sipping a cup of coffee. When she saw me, she lifted her mug and smiled as I walked past her to the Keurig machine. I doctored up my brew as usual, with plenty of French vanilla creamer and a few packets of sugar. I sat down in my familiar spot on the couch and got comfortable. It felt good. It felt normal, something I haven't experienced a lot of since Chuck died. Unfortunately, my contentment was short-lived.

"I have some news to share with you." She said through a huge smile; she was practically glowing with happiness.

"You're pregnant?!" I guessed with enthusiasm.

She laughed and shook her head.

"No, not that I'm aware of!"

"But you're right about it being related to family; Brian and I have decided to move back east to be near our relatives.

So, I'm afraid this is going to be our last session." She had "no big deal" kind of tone to her voice.

I sat there speechless and just stared at her. My last little scrap of normality flew out the window. Never before had I felt so helpless and alone. There was no escape, no one else to turn to. My face must have been telling her quite a story.

"What are you thinking? Are you OK?" I could tell the concern in her voice was genuine.

"I guess I'm going to have to be," I told her through a forced smile.

I didn't say much the rest of our session. I let her do all the talking. Most of the time I was somewhere else, I could hear her words, but they sounded like they were coming from another world.

I thought mostly about Chuck, practically replaying our entire friendship in my mind. I thought about the last time I was at his apartment and closed the door behind me for good.

* * *

Percy and I were seeing the light at the end of the tunnel. We had all Chuck's belongings packed in boxes and taped shut. I was wiping down the kitchen and Percy was vacuuming, when the doorbell rang. Percy turned off the machine and went to answer the door. He put his hand on the knob and hesitated, turning to me.

"I didn't know Chuck had a doorbell?" He asked.

"I didn't either…" I said with a shrug, then I snickered, causing him to do the same.

He opened the door and let two Salvation Army men

into the apartment. Next thing we knew, they were gone, and we were standing in an empty shell that used to be Chuck's world.

"I'm gonna go now," Percy told me, his voice was hollow and weak.

"Thank you so much for your help. I don't think I could have done it without you." My voice shook, and my throat tightened as I tried to hold back the tears.

We hugged for a long moment; then he walked out the door without looking back. It was the last time I would ever see Percy.

I did a final walkthrough, not to make sure we didn't miss something, but because I couldn't bring myself to leave. It was strange because at the same time I couldn't bear to be there anymore. But before I could leave, I decided I needed to say goodbye.

"Everything is done here Chuck. Thank you for being the best friend anybody could ever ask for; I'm going to miss you forever. And I wanted to tell you that I changed my mind about something. Remember talking about whether we would go back in time and change anything about our lives, if we could? Remember I said no, I didn't regret anything, and I didn't want to change a thing, good or bad? Well, I was wrong. I would go back to the night of that stupid New Year's Eve party, and I would make sure to stop you from going somehow. I know it wouldn't have been easy. Even if I had to tie you up, I'd keep you at home that night. And by the way, I don't think I ever told you before, but I love you."

I turned the lock on the door and stepped outside. I stood

holding the nob for several minutes, dreading shutting it for the very last time.

* * *

When I finally found myself back in the moment, I looked up, and Doctor Kelley was watching me in silence. Then she smiled.

"You may not think so right now, but you're gonna be OK. You have your family; this would be a good time to lean on them."

I nodded in agreement and allowed myself one last visual scan of her office. Honestly, I had no idea how sentimental I was until all this happened.

I stood up from the couch for the last time, and set my coffee cup on her desk, also for the last time. I was starting to feel pretty sorry for myself again, when I noticed a box on the floor. It was full of all the stuff Doctor Kelley had packed so far. She was moving away... what a great idea. It came to me just like that. I would move to California and live with Joy in her brand-new big house. I would get a pet carrier and leave Missoula with the only friend I had left here. I could feel a slight smile cross my face. Doctor Kelley noticed it and questioned my change of expression.

"I'm gonna go live with my sister." She placed a soft hand on my cheek,

"I'm glad." Her smile was genuine.

Leaving her office for the last time was a bittersweet experience. Our hands were clasped tightly together as we wished each other well for the rest of our lives. We knew this would be the last time we ever saw each other. I walked out of the building, and onto the street with a renewed sense of hope.

CHAPTER 43

MOVING DAY

I decided I needed to make a clean break from this place. There wasn't going to be anything but Boyd, my tattered suitcase, and myself on the airplane to California. I packed up the apartment into a million manageable-sized boxes and called the Salvation Army one more time. Anything else we needed we would buy after settling into Joy's place. It was an exciting feeling to be starting anew, and admittedly quite scary, or maybe it was a combination. I think that would be called exhilarating.

Did you know that cats can sense things? That the sheer sight of an animal carrier can turn them into maniacal idiots? Well, it's true. It was far from easy, and I won't go into the gory details, but I finally got Boyd trapped into his travel vessel, where he would remain until we got to Joy's house.

We waited in the doorway of our boxed-up apartment for the cab to the airport. Boyd howled nervously from his carrier, as I gave the place we called home for so long one last look around. I didn't want a repeat of my behavior after packing up and getting ready to leave Chuck's place. I couldn't go through that again, so I talked myself out of it. I told myself it was only a few rooms, the memories from the events that took place there are what mattered, and they were going with me. I thought about all the great times that took place and all the bullshit. I wouldn't trade a minute of either for anything. My nostalgic, melancholy, and probably romanticized trip down memory lane was interrupted by the obnoxious blast of the taxi's horn. With my suitcase in one hand, and my best friend in the other, it was a serious struggle climbing the stairs. I realized by sheer weight alone, that I had much more cat than I had stuff.

I opened the back door of the cab and set Boyd on the seat. I got into the front with the driver, and we headed out. The cabby commented on Boyd's mood. I guess not everyone enjoys the deafening sounds of an outraged cat.

I stared out the window and noticed every establishment I had ever patronized go quickly passed the taxi. There was a treasured or regretful memory for each one we left in our wake. I wondered if I would ever be in Missoula again. I couldn't imagine why I would. It's always weird when things come to an end. I remember Percy and Chuck talking about it once not long ago. Percy wondered what the last song he would ever hear would be. It made me wonder what Chuck's last song was.

We instantly felt at home. Joy introduced us to our new bedroom. It was spacious and tastefully decorated. It came complete with a king-size bed, 65-inch television set, and an attached ensuite. I got us all set up, my suitcase was emptied, and I filled a litter box full of sand for Boyd in our bathroom, which he took advantage of before I could get the lid back on the jug. He followed me to the kitchen and had his first meal as a Californian. Then he decided it was time to explore; he sniffed every inch of the house, after which he took a nap on our new bed. I think he liked it here, that made me quite happy.

Joy walked me around the property, and I got acquainted with my new surroundings.

"You must be starving; let's go to the store." She suggested with a smile.

We picked out a couple of monster rib-eye steaks and a plastic bag full of readymade salad, which included a packet of ranch dressing and about five croutons in a tiny cellophane wrapper. We drank a few bottles of bud light and hit the sack early.

The move to California was exactly what I needed. I felt a sense of peace that I had almost forgotten existed. I'm pretty sure our being in the house was just as beneficial for Joy. I could tell she was doing much better and was well into her healing process. Not long after Kyle died, she began volunteering at a cancer care facility. She said it was the best thing she ever did. She also joined a local church and has met some very nice people. They have a support group for folks who have recently lost loved ones. She invited me to join. I wasn't a support group kind of person, but I thanked her anyway. I did have plans of my own, however. I would be seeking out a new therapist in the very near future.

CHAPTER 44

DOCTOR MORGAN

Doctor Morgan's office was nothing like Doctor Kelley's. It was in a newly constructed business complex, and still smelled of fresh paint and newly laid industrial carpet. Doctor Kelley's office smelled of ancient cigarette smoke, coffee grounds and musty old books, which I somehow preferred.

I sat and waited for my new Doctor while trying to relax in a large designer chair that practically screamed Pottery Barn. I scanned the room. There was no dust on the blinds and everything on the shelves looked perfect and staged. I wondered if the books on them were real or props. There was no coffee pot, no French Vanilla Creamer, and no sugar packets. I think I was trying to convince myself that this was a bad idea. I had to get over believing Doctor Kelley was the only qualified therapist in the world. I needed to quit being so immature. I knew I should just sit tight and give this a shot. Besides, if it didn't work out, I could always find another therapist in an old shitty, dirty building further downtown. Or maybe I just didn't wanna do therapy anymore at all. Did I have the strength to start at the beginning again? His entrance interrupted my silent idiocies.

He looked to be a man in his mid to late 50s. He was tall and thin, with dark greasy looking hair parted sharply to one side. His face was covered in thick-rimmed glasses, a very sculpted mustache, and a stoic expression. I couldn't imagine there being anything close to a sense of humor in that package. I decided I didn't like him before he even opened his mouth. Within a few minutes, I would be reminded why you shouldn't judge a book by its cover.

He bypassed his desk and headed straight for me. His hand was extended, and his stoic look disappeared, replaced by a smile, which could only be described as welcoming and sincere.

"Hello, I'm Doctor Jacob Morgan, but please call me Jake. I'm not much for formalities."

"Nice to meet you, Jake." I said, accepting his handshake. "I'm Lisa Jenkins."

www.ingramcontent.com/pod-product-compliance
Lightning Source LLC
Chambersburg PA
CBHW072108300726
48975CB00003B/750

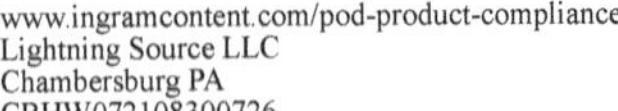